W9-AXG-481

JOINING THE CLUB

"You'll need to put in hours and hours of practice each day," Tori said, "especially if you want to improve on that sitspin you did a few minutes ago."

"What was wrong with it?" Nikki asked.

Tori looked directly at Nikki. "It's just my opinion, but I think you need to work on your form. You look kind of awkward and amateurish when you spin."

"I don't think so," Jill said. "I think Nikki has a great sitspin."

Tori shrugged. "All I know is what I saw," she said. Then she turned and skated back to the corner of the rink.

What's her problem? Nikki wondered as she watched Tori go. Just a minute ago Nikki had been feeling lucky because she'd made some fast friends. Now it seemed as though she'd made an enemy too.

Silver Blades

titles in Large-Print Editions:

BREAKING
THE ICE

~ ~

Melissa Lowell

Created by Parachute Press

Gareth Stevens Publishing
MILWAUKEE

For a free color catalog describing Gareth Stevens' list of high-quality books and multimedia programs, call 1-800-542-2595 (USA) or 1-800-461-9120 (Canada). Gareth Stevens Publishing's Fax: (414) 225-0377. See our catalog, too, on the World Wide Web: http://gsinc.com

Library of Congress Cataloging-in-Publication Data

Lowell, Melissa.
    Breaking the ice / Melissa Lowell.
        p. cm. — (Silver blades; #1)
    Summary: Nikki is admitted into a prestigious ice skating club where the competition is really tough and one of the other skaters considers Nikki a threat to her status.
    ISBN 0-8368-2063-0 (lib. bdg.)
    [1. Ice skating—Fiction. 2. Competition—Fiction.]
    I. Title. II. Series: Lowell, Melissa. Silver blades; #1.
    PZ7.L96456Br 1998
    [Fic]—dc21   97-39601

First published in this edition in 1998 by
Gareth Stevens Publishing
1555 North RiverCenter Drive, Suite 201
Milwaukee, WI 53212 USA

© 1993 by Parachute Press, Inc. Cover art by Bart Bemus/Bill Garland. Published by arrangement with Bantam Doubleday Dell Books for Young Readers, a division of Bantam Doubleday Dell Publishing Group, Inc., New York, New York. All rights reserved.

Printed in the United States of America

1 2 3 4 5 6 7 8 9 02 01 00 99 98

1

Nikki Simon stepped out onto the huge, gleaming ice rink. Fans from around the world watched in silence as she began her routine for the Olympic finals. She glided across the ice, flawlessly performing every jump and spin she'd practiced for years. Slowly Nikki built momentum for the most difficult part of her routine—the triple axel jump. Only a few women in the world had ever completed the jump in competition. So far no one had done it that afternoon, and if Nikki could, she would win the gold medal.

Nikki lifted her left foot, then sprang into the air, twisting three times before landing on her right foot again. She'd made it! The fans leapt to their feet, and the crowd's cheering was deafening. Nikki held a dramatic finishing pose in the center of the rink as flowers rained down from the bleachers and blanketed the ice. She turned toward the judges and dropped into a graceful curtsy. Then, skating off the ice, she turned to wave to her fans—

"All right if I just drop you off today?"

Startled out of her daydream, Nikki turned to her mother, sitting in the car beside her. Mrs. Simon stopped the car in front of the Seneca Hills Ice Arena. "I've still got so much unpacking to do."

"I don't mind, Mom. I wouldn't want you to sit around here for four hours. I'll see you later." Nikki gave her mother a quick kiss before getting out of the car.

Nikki stared at the modern Seneca Hills Ice Arena with its stark white exterior. The sun glinted off the glass doors of the main entrance. The building had only a few small windows in front and was surrounded by neatly trimmed grass. Even though Nikki had been to the arena several times before, it still impressed her. It was at least five times as large as the rink where she used to skate back home in Missouri. Seneca Hills was where she hoped to begin her training for the Olympics.

Nikki still couldn't believe she was here. She had moved to Seneca Hills, Pennsylvania, just three weeks ago to try to join Silver Blades, one of the most exclusive skating clubs in the country. There were only about twenty-five members in the club, and tryouts were being held this Monday. If Nikki made it, she'd have the chance to train with some of the best skaters and coaches in the country.

Nikki quickly made her way toward the ice rink to the right of the lobby. There were two Olympic-sized ice rinks in the arena, one on each side of the locker rooms, which were directly across from the main doors. Down a long hallway off the lobby were a snack bar, pro shop, and weight room.

Nikki was already wearing her practice clothes— leggings, a white T-shirt, and a sweatshirt. Nikki was thin with green eyes and brown hair, braces on her teeth, and freckles sprinkled across her nose. She sat down on the bottom level of a row of bleachers to put on her skates. About twelve skaters were on the ice, warming up with jumps and spins. A popular dance song was playing over the loudspeaker. This was a freestyle session, which meant that serious skaters paid extra money to have the rink to themselves without the distractions of a crowd. Nikki wanted to work on her jumps as much as she could before the tryouts in three days.

She pulled her skates out of her bag and slipped her feet into the stiff leather boots. This pair was still fairly new; Nikki's feet had been growing quite a bit, and it seemed that between changing sizes and skating so much, she was buying a new pair every few months now. Bending over, she quickly began to lace her skates. She wanted to get on the ice before it became too chopped up by the other skaters' blades. Nikki glanced sideways as a girl sat down on the bench next to her and began putting on her own skates.

Nikki had seen the girl at school and on the ice a few times before. She was a beautiful skater with a very dramatic presence. Her moves were smooth and lyrical. She had very long, straight black hair that fell to the middle of her back. Nikki thought the girl's face, with its Asian features and dark, solemn eyes, was beautiful. But what Nikki had noticed most of all was that the girl always wore something red. Today she had on a red skating dress, a red zippered sweater, and a red headband.

"Hi," the girl said, noticing Nikki's gaze. "You're new, aren't you?"

Nikki smiled. This was the first time that anyone at the rink had spoken to her. "Yeah, I am new," she said. "I just moved here, actually. My name's Nikki Simon."

"I'm Jill Wong," the girl said, smiling back at her. "Are you going to try out for Silver Blades?"

Nikki nodded. "Are you in the club?"

"Yes," Jill said. "Three years."

"Wow," replied Nikki. "You know, I think we're in the same social studies class. Do you have Mrs. Cone, second period?"

"You mean Mrs. Conehead, the Human Sleeping Pill?" Jill grinned.

Nikki laughed. "She *is* pretty boring."

"Boring? Deadly is more like it." Jill tied her skate

laces into a double knot. "The only way I can stay awake is by rehearsing spins and jumps in my head while she talks."

"You do that too?" Nikki commented. "I thought I was the only one who was going over skating moves in the middle of that filmstrip on the Civil War."

Jill laughed. "We're going to be in big trouble if she ever calls on us."

"I know," Nikki said. "But maybe I'll be able to pay attention after the tryouts. That is, if I make the club."

"I've watched you skate," Jill said. "You're good— I think you'll make it."

"Really?" Nikki said.

Jill nodded. "Absolutely. How long have you been skating?" She stood up and headed toward the ice.

"Four years," Nikki said, following Jill. "How about you?"

"Five," Jill said. "For the first two years I didn't take it very seriously. But since I joined this club, it's become my whole life. Everyone works really hard to prepare for competitions and elaborate ice shows. There's practice at five forty-five every morning, ballet classes, weight lifting . . ."

"I know it's a lot of work," Nikki said. "But I'm ready for it."

Only seventy-two more hours until tryouts, she thought, stepping onto the ice after Jill. Then I'll find out once and for all if I'm good enough to be in

Silver Blades. Nikki was going to put everything she had into making the club. Her parents had sacrificed a lot for her skating, and more than anything, Nikki wanted to make her dream of being in the Olympics come true.

"Hi, Kara. Come on in," Nikki said as she opened her front door. She was surprised to find Kara Logan standing on her front steps at ten o'clock on Saturday morning. Kara was one of the most popular girls in the seventh grade at Grandview Middle School, and even though she lived next door to Nikki, Nikki hadn't expected to become her friend so easily.

Kara was wearing blue jeans with a silver belt, a white shirt, and her blond hair was pulled back into a ponytail. As usual, Kara looked very cool. Nikki had met Kara a little over two weeks ago on the first day of school. It hadn't taken Nikki long to realize that Kara and her friends were the cool group. Kids stopped by Kara's table in the cafeteria, but never sat down unless they were invited. Kara and her friends seemed to be the leaders of most after-school clubs or sports. And Kara's group had an equal number of boys and girls in it, which in Nikki's opinion was a sure sign of popularity. Kara was nice, but she was so sure of herself that Nikki sometimes felt shy around her.

"This is a great house," Kara said, looking around

the living room. "I'm *so* glad you live here now instead of the obnoxious boys who did before. They were a nightmare. They went to Kent Academy and they thought they were so great." Kara stuck her nose up in the air. "Total snobs."

Nikki laughed. "Want to see my room?"

"Sure." Kara followed Nikki upstairs. "Don't you love Saturdays? What are you doing today?"

Nikki walked into her bedroom. "Waiting for my mom to get home so she can take me to the ice rink. There's a freestyle session at noon that I want to go to."

"You're going to practice again?" said Kara. "All you ever do is ice-skate. Wait a second—I think I see why." She looked around Nikki's room. There were rows of shelves covered with tiny skating figurines. Every birthday and Christmas her parents surprised Nikki with a new addition to her collection. Some figurines were made of china, some were ceramic, and others were made of glass. They were all of skaters posed in graceful positions.

Nikki suddenly realized just how many mementos of her figure skating she had. In the corner on the floor was a stack of back issues of her favorite magazine, *Skating*. Taped to the inside of her closet door were dozens of pictures and articles about Nancy Kerrigan, Kristi Yamaguchi, and other championship skaters.

"I guess you can tell that I love to skate," Nikki said with a shrug.

"I'll say." Kara shook her head. "Hey, who's this?"

She pointed to a framed photo on the wall. "He's cute."

"Oh, that's Tom, one of my best friends from home," Nikki said. She pointed to two other photos. "And that's Katy, and that's Erica. We all worked on the student council together." Nikki couldn't believe how much she missed her friends back home. Even though Katy and Erica had written and called a lot since Nikki had moved, it just wasn't the same.

"Do you think they'll ever come visit?" Kara asked, still examining Tom's picture.

"I hope so," Nikki replied. "I really miss them."

Kara sat down on Nikki's bed. "So how often do you practice? It seems like every time I talk to you, you're about to go to the rink."

"Didn't I tell you? Tryouts for Silver Blades are Monday," Nikki said.

"Silver Blades—the skating club? I think Jamie Ross skates there. It's supposed to be a big deal, isn't it?" asked Kara.

"It's one of the best figure-skating clubs in the country," Nikki said, her green eyes wide with excitement. "And it's really competitive."

"Wow." Kara was noticeably impressed. "You must be a really good skater."

"Not yet," Nikki said. "But I want to go to the Olympics someday. We actually moved here so I could join Silver Blades."

"You're kidding," Kara said. "My parents would never do something like that. I can't believe your family moved just so you could ice-skate!"

"Well, it wasn't *only* for my ice-skating," answered Nikki. She sat in her desk chair backward so she faced Kara. "My father's company wanted him to transfer, and the Pennsylvania office was one of his choices. The ice rink I used to skate at in Missouri was small and run-down. There really weren't many kids who took skating seriously there. My coach, Eloise, told my mom and dad that if I wanted to be a serious figure skater, I'd have to find another rink, with more specialized training. So Eloise suggested a bunch of skating clubs—one of them was Silver Blades."

"What happens if you don't make Silver Blades?" asked Kara. "Not to bring up a bad subject or anything."

Nikki was silent for a moment. She had spent all summer trying to push that possibility from her mind. "I don't know. I guess I'll have to give up on the Olympics," she said finally.

"Well, I bet you'll make it. Your parents must think so, right?" said Kara. "Listen, I came over here to ask you something. Wendy, Craig, Jeff, Jenny, and I are planning the big fall dance at school. Do you want to help?"

"Sure." Nikki was thrilled to be included.

"Great. We're all getting together at the mall around one today to get ideas for decorations and music," Kara said. "Can you meet us there?"

Nikki sighed. "No, I won't be finished with my practice until after two o'clock."

"Oh. Well, how about coming over to my house on Thursday afternoon? We're having an official committee meeting then," said Kara.

"Can it be Thursday night, after dinner?" Nikki asked. She didn't want to be difficult, but she would have skating practice every day after school—if she made the club.

"Sure—no problem," Kara said, smiling. "So how do you like Grandview so far?" She picked up one of the figurines and gave it a closer look.

Nikki shrugged. "It's going pretty well. I guess I'm still a little homesick."

"Hey, if *I* were friends with that guy Tom, I'd be homesick too," Kara said, raising her eyebrows at Nikki. Then she laughed. "But seriously. There's tons of stuff to do in Seneca Hills. I bet you're going to like it here."

"I'm sure I will," Nikki said, nodding. It was nice to have someone as friendly as Kara welcome her to town.

"Okay." Kara put the figurine back and lay down on the bed. "The *first* thing you have to know is all the Grandview gossip."

Nikki grinned. "Go ahead. Tell me everything!"

2

Nikki's heart was pounding as she and her mother walked into the arena on Monday afternoon. The lobby was packed with skaters. At her practice sessions over the past three weeks only about fifteen skaters had been on the ice. Now there were over a hundred in the lobby. Where had all these skaters come from? Nikki wondered as she gazed at girls of every imaginable age, shape, and size. There were also about twenty boys. Nikki had heard that there were only seven spots open in the club, but she hadn't known that she'd be competing against this many skaters. Even her mother looked astonished.

Weaving through all the skaters and their parents, Mrs. Simon led Nikki to the registration table that had been set up in the middle of the lobby.

"Name?" asked one of the women working at the table.

"Nikki Simon." Nikki nervously ran her tongue over her braces.

The woman began searching through a plastic file. "Here we are," she said, handing an index card to Mrs. Simon. "We need some more information before you can go into the tryouts. If you'll just fill out this card." Mrs. Simon took the card, and the woman turned her attention to the skater standing behind Nikki.

While Mrs. Simon filled out the card, Nikki shifted her bag to her other shoulder and moved out of the line. Every time the door to the figure-skating rink opened, strains of music drifted out and skaters hurried through.

Nikki was so busy watching the parade of figure skaters that she didn't notice the two hockey players until it was too late.

"Heads up!" one boy cried just before he bumped into her, knocking her skating bag off her arm and onto the floor. "Sorry," he mumbled. He was covered from head to toe in hockey gear and was carrying several hockey sticks. The other hockey player, who was wearing a jersey that said Seneca Hills Hawks, picked up Nikki's bag and handed it to her without saying a word. He was tall and broad-shouldered, with brown hair and a summer tan. He paused for a moment and gave Nikki a smile. Then he followed his friend into the rink to the left of the lobby, where hockey practice was being held.

"Okay, Nikki, you're all set," Mrs. Simon said, coming up to her. "Your turn is coming up in about twenty minutes. They're trying people out on a first-come, first-served basis. Why don't you go change?"

Nikki nodded and went across the hall into the locker room. Her hands were trembling so much, it was nearly impossible to zip her skating dress up the back, but she finally managed it. Think positively, she told herself as she checked her reflection in the mirror. She had on her favorite emerald-green skating dress with a matching clip in her hair, flesh-colored tights, and a white warm-up jacket. You can do it.

She went back to the lobby and handed her skating bag to her mother. "Okay, I'm ready," she said. Together they walked toward the rink.

A blast of cold, dry air hit Nikki's face as she opened the heavy door. Inside, classical music was playing over the loudspeaker, and the people in the bleachers were watching in hushed silence as a boy dressed in black skated.

"I see a spot over there." Her mother pointed toward the middle of the bleachers.

As Nikki followed, she watched the skater perform a simple spin. Standing close to him on the ice were a man and a woman. Probably the judges, Nikki thought, and she felt her stomach flutter.

The bleachers were filled with skaters and their parents, all waiting their turn. At the very top of the bleachers was a group of about twenty kids wearing light-blue warm-up jackets with SILVER BLADES written in white. Nikki hadn't realized that the members of the club would be watching her try out too. Somehow that seemed even scarier than having the judges stand so close to her while she skated. Nikki sat down and took her white figure skates out of her skating bag. Slowly she began to lace them. As her fingers worked, her eyes focused on the ice, where a blond girl in a pink dress was now trying out. Her sense of balance seemed a little off to Nikki. The skater circled the ice once and began an axel, one and a half rotations in the air, from a forward takeoff. But the girl had barely completed one rotation before she fell. That could be me in a few minutes, Nikki thought, watching the girl scramble to her feet.

"Don't watch the other skaters," her mother advised. "It'll only make you nervous. Why don't you listen to your tape and stretch? Try to block out everything else."

"Good idea," said Nikki, fishing her Walkman out of her bag. As her mother left to get a cup of hot coffee from the snack bar, Nikki did some stretching exercises. Then she draped an old fuzzy blanket over her legs to keep her muscles warm. She started digging through her bag for the special tape that her friend Katy had made for her. Nikki listened to the tape before every competition or performance. It was a collection of her favorite songs. In the past Katy had come to all of her competitions, and Nikki wished she were at the rink now, to make her laugh and help her relax. Katy couldn't skate at all—she was a total

klutz—but she was great at making party mix tapes.
"Hi there!"

Nikki looked up to see Jill Wong standing before her. Jill was wearing red leggings, a white sweatshirt with a red silhouette of a figure skater printed on it, and her Silver Blades jacket. There were two other girls with her.

"Hi." Nikki smiled.

"We thought we'd come down and give you some moral support. You know, sort of be your own private cheerleaders," said Jill, jumping up and down.

"Thanks," said Nikki. "I can use all the help I can get."

Jill gestured to her friends. "This is Danielle Panati and Tori Carsen. They're the only other seventh-graders in Silver Blades besides me. Danielle goes to Grandview with us."

"What about you?" Nikki asked Tori. "Do you go to Grandview too?"

Tori was short and petite, with blue eyes and curly blond hair. She was wearing a dark-blue patterned sweater and black stirrup pants. She shook her head. "I go to Kent. It's a private school in Burgess." Burgess was the next town over from Seneca Hills. "But my best friends go to Grandview," Tori said, smiling.

"What best friends?" Danielle grinned. "You mean—us?" Danielle had shoulder-length honey-brown hair and large brown eyes, and she wasn't quite as thin as the other girls. She was wearing a white skating skirt and the light-blue-and-white Silver Blades warm-up jacket, and she was holding a large science textbook.

"You'd never know it from her jokes, but Danielle's a brain," said Jill. "That textbook is permanently attached to her arm. If she isn't skating, she's studying."

"That's not true!" Danielle protested. "Jill's just allergic to homework."

"No, I'm not," Jill said. "I just don't like it very much, that's all."

They all laughed.

Danielle looked at Nikki. "Good luck with your tryout. I still remember how scary it is. I only became a member last year."

"I just hope I don't fall," Nikki said. "If they ask me to do anything like a double flip, I'm in big trouble. I've been trying forever to land that jump."

"Me too," said Danielle. "But don't worry. So far only Jill has landed it, among the three of us."

"I'm going to get it soon," Tori said in a determined voice. "Anyway, falling's not such a big deal. I fell during my tryout," Tori admitted. "But I *was* only eight years old at the time."

"Big help you are," Jill retorted sarcastically. "Listen, Nikki, don't sweat it. I've seen lots of skaters audition today, and I don't think any of them is as good as you. You've been practicing a lot—I'm sure you'll do fine."

"Thanks," said Nikki. She really appreciated Jill's confidence in her.

Just then a little girl with black braids sticking straight out from either side of her head ran up and grabbed Jill's hand. "Can we get something to eat?"

"This is Randi, my sister," Jill explained. "I have six younger brothers and sisters, so I usually get stuck baby-sitting one of them after school."

"Sounds like fun," said Nikki enviously. "I'm an only child. I'd love to have a little sister."

Randi began jumping up and down, whining about being hungry, and Jill sighed. "She's all yours—anytime you want. Come on, Randi—I have some apples up in my skating bag."

Jill, Tori, and Danielle wished Nikki luck again and then, taking Jill's little sister with them, headed back up toward the top row of bleachers. Nikki felt much calmer. She was happy to know someone besides her mother was rooting for her.

She could see her mother making her way back to their seat. A tall girl was skating off the ice in tears. Nikki wondered what had happened. The loudspeaker crackled, and "Nikki Simon, next" echoed throughout the rink.

Nikki could feel her heart beating wildly. Her knees were shaking as she stood up. The judges were holding their clipboards and waiting for her alongside the rink.

Nikki's mother squeezed her hand in support as she took Nikki's warm-up jacket from her. Nikki removed the rubber guards from her skates and took a deep breath as she stepped onto the ice.

This is it, she told herself. It's all up to me now.

3

Nikki began to glide around the rink, taking long, fluid strokes. She leaned into her skating leg and pushed off with her free leg, slowly building speed.

To warm up, Nikki circled the rink several times, gaining more power with each trip around. Then she did a quick turn and began skating backward, crossing one foot over the other. The skirt of her skating dress billowed in the breeze, and she felt her body start to relax as her feet performed the familiar motions. Finally she felt ready to approach the two judges.

"Hello, Nikki," a short, balding man said with a slight German accent. "I am Mr. Weiler, one of the coaches of Silver Blades."

Nikki knew exactly who he was. Anyone who loved skating as much as she did knew that Franz Weiler had won a silver medal in the Olympics in the 1960s.

19

He had been a great skater then and was now known to be a terrific coach. He was one of the reasons Eloise had suggested Silver Blades to Nikki.

Mr. Weiler pointed to the young woman standing next to him. "And this is Kathy Bart. She also coaches Silver Blades."

"Hi, Nikki," Kathy said. She seemed to be in her late twenties, and her long, dark-blond hair was pulled back in a ponytail. Nikki knew that several years before, Kathy had placed fourth in the Nationals, the highest-level figure-skating competition in the United States. The top three skaters in the Nationals went on to the World Competition or to the Olympics.

"Okay, Nikki, we're going to ask you to perform a series of jumps, spins, and footwork. These moves will be done without music. Sometimes we'll ask to see something twice. You should just do everything to the best of your ability," instructed Mr. Weiler. "Let's start with a camel spin."

Relieved, Nikki skated toward the center of the rink. The camel was one of her better spins. She had never understood what it had to do with a camel, though, since the spin involved spinning on one foot while the other foot was raised in an arabesque.

Nikki made a small circle with backward crossovers around the center of the rink and readied herself for the spin. *Focus. Focus.* She repeated the words over and over in her mind.

She stepped into the spin with her left foot and whipped her body around quickly to gain speed and momentum. She raised her right leg and arched her back gracefully. Pulling both arms back so that her body was one fluid line, she concentrated on centering the spin. She knew the judges would be looking at the markings left on the ice by the edge of her skate blade. If the spin was done well, the markings would all be centered around one small tight circle. But if the scratchings on the ice showed curlicues spiraling away from the center, the judges would know that she had traveled in her spin.

After about ten rotations Nikki lowered her right leg and brought her foot quickly in toward her left knee. She pulled her arms in hard and, at the same time, moved her right foot straight down toward the ice. This rapid motion gave her the power to turn very fast. She finished with a magnificent scratch spin.

Nikki held her ending position for a moment. She smiled, knowing that the camel spin was right on the mark. But the coaches weren't about to stop her tryout for any congratulations.

"Show me a flip jump into a loop jump!" Kathy called out.

Again Nikki circled the ice, taking a few minutes to concentrate on the combinations, imagining in her mind how the jumps would look. Then she leapt high in the air. Twisting and turning, she completed both maneuvers.

"Next give us an axel jump."

"Do a change-foot sitspin."

"One more time."

"Try a double-toe loop."

Nikki was in constant motion, performing jumps and spins, one after the other. She was so focused on the tryout that she was no longer aware of her mother, or Jill, Danielle, and Tori, watching her from the bleachers. She had blocked out everything except her own movements and the sound of the judges' voices. Beads of perspiration dotted her brow, making her bangs curl.

"Okay, Nikki. Now I want to see a split jump," Mr. Weiler commanded.

Nikki skated rapidly around the ice. Suddenly she hit her toe pick into the ice with incredible force, and she launched her body high in the air. Then she extended both legs out to the sides in a split, straightening her knees as she did. The jump lasted only a second. The instant Nikki touched back down on the solid ice, she knew she had landed the jump perfectly.

Breathing heavily, Nikki turned toward the judges. Kathy and Mr. Weiler were both furiously scribbling something on their clipboards. Nikki was dying to know what they were writing.

Kathy skated over to Nikki. "Now I'm going to show you a short footwork pattern made up mostly of different edges and turns," she explained. "The footwork should be performed in time to the music that'll play over the loudspeaker in a minute or two."

Nikki nodded. She knew that she was being tested to see how fast she could pick up choreography. She had been taking ballet lessons for the past few years to help with her skating program, so she was used to receiving sequences of steps and memorizing them.

Nikki watched as Kathy patiently showed her the pattern. Despite her bulky blue sweater, Kathy's turns looked sharp and clean. Every movement was precise.

Nikki kept careful count in her head as Kathy went over the pattern a second time. Turn. Turn. Crossover. Glide. Turn.

"Now let's see what you can do," Kathy said. She skated back toward Mr. Weiler.

Nikki looked around, perplexed. She wasn't quite sure what she was supposed to do until the music started.

Noticing her confusion, Kathy called out, "Skate to the center of the rink! Wait for the music to play and then start the footwork pattern."

Nikki got into position and took a deep breath. Out of the corner of her eye she could see both judges standing in different spots on the ice. They wanted to be able to watch her footwork from different angles. Nikki waited for the music to begin. She felt as if she were under a microscope—she had never had anyone watch her skate so closely before.

The loudspeaker crackled. The music began. One, and two, and three, and four, and . . . Nikki counted the beats in her head, trying to stay in time with the music. She pulled her shoulders back and attempted to keep her head up. It wasn't easy not to watch her feet.

Imitating the rapid edges and turns was very difficult. Nikki got halfway through the pattern when she suddenly lost count. Had she done three sets of mohawk turns or four? She fumbled her step.

Just before she was about to give up and ask for help, Nikki heard a refrain of the music that she recognized. Quickly she got back into sync. Turning onto an inside edge, she finished the straight-line pattern.

When the music stopped, Nikki looked anxiously at Kathy and Mr. Weiler. She knew she hadn't given her strongest performance.

But their faces remained expressionless. "One last jump and you'll be done," Mr. Weiler boomed.

"Let's see a double flip," Kathy said.

Nikki felt her stomach tighten. She couldn't believe it. She'd just finished telling Jill and the other girls that she couldn't do this jump, and now Kathy wanted to see it. Nikki was about to explain she still hadn't mastered the double flip, when abruptly she changed her mind. If she wanted to place in competitions, she'd have to perform lots of difficult jumps. Landing the double flip would eventually be essential to her career.

Nikki nodded at Kathy, then closed her eyes for a second and focused on the double flip: It required a backward takeoff from her toe pick and then two full revolutions high in the air, landing cleanly on one foot. She could do it—she knew she could. In the past she'd always performed well under pressure.

Nikki rounded the rink, concentrating on building

power with her backward crossovers. She prepared to jump and dug her toe pick into the ice. A split second later she was high in the air. She pulled her arms in tight and quickly spun around and around. After two full rotations she landed cleanly—on her rear end.

Nikki quickly got to her feet and forced herself to smile at Kathy and Mr. Weiler.

"Thank you very much, Nikki," Mr. Weiler said. "You may go now."

"We'll let you know tomorrow," Kathy said, making some final notations on the sheet on her clipboard.

Nikki skated back over to the edge of the rink, trying to hide her dismay. Why did I have to fall on my last jump? she thought. That's all the judges are going to remember!

"Do you want any more potatoes, Nikki?" Mrs. Simon asked that night at dinner.

"No, thanks," Nikki mumbled. She'd barely eaten anything on her plate. Her mother had insisted she come down for dinner, but all Nikki wanted to do was hide in her bedroom. She wasn't hungry. She couldn't stop thinking about how she had blown her only chance to get into Silver Blades. She would have to wait another six months to try again—tryouts were held only twice a year.

"*I'll* have some more potatoes," Nikki's father said.

Mrs. Simon shook her head. "No, you won't. You're supposed to be on a diet, remember? Have some more broccoli instead."

"Great. Just what I was craving." Mr. Simon winked at Nikki. Her father was always on some kind of diet that he hated. So far he hadn't stuck to any of them. Normally Nikki would have given him a hard time about it, but tonight she just wasn't in the mood.

"Honey, I know what you're thinking, but not eating won't change anything. All we can do now is wait until the tryout results are posted tomorrow afternoon," Mrs. Simon said.

"Niks, you have to be optimistic," added Nikki's father. "I'm sure you'll make the club. Your mother told me you did wonderfully except for that fall."

Nikki tried to smile so that her father would stop looking so worried. He was always telling her to look on the bright side. Usually she appreciated his optimism, but tonight it wasn't what she needed to hear.

She stood up to clear her plate from the table. She was halfway to the kitchen when the telephone rang. Maybe it's one of my friends from home, Nikki thought hopefully. Katy knew tryouts were today.

"I'll get it," she told her parents, hurrying toward the phone mounted on the kitchen wall. "Hello?"

"Hi, Nikki. It's Jill Wong. How's it going?"

"Not so great," Nikki replied, setting her plate full of food on the counter.

"How come? Is your rear end still frozen solid?" Jill teased.

"Jill, I can't believe I did that," Nikki said. "I blew the whole tryout!"

"Come on, Nikki, lighten up!" Jill urged. "You didn't blow it—you did fine."

"Thanks, but you don't have to say that. I fell, and that's all there is to it," Nikki said in a dejected voice, twisting the phone cord around her finger. "There's no way they'll let me into the club now."

"No, you're wrong," Jill argued. "You fell while doing the hardest jump anyone tried all day. Most kids weren't even asked to *try* a double flip!"

"So?" Nikki asked.

"So, it's amazing you went for it the way you did. Most kids would have held back and barely gotten the jump off the ice."

"That doesn't mean I'll make the club," Nikki said.

"I can see I'm not going to convince you," Jill said. "Listen, I've been in Silver Blades for three years and I only landed that jump a little while ago. Danielle can't do one. And even Tori, who never compliments any-one but herself, was totally amazed by your tryout. I mean, she was speechless. For Tori to admit someone else is good on the ice—that's proof enough you did a good job."

"Really? Tori thought I was good?" Nikki couldn't help smiling a little.

"We *all* thought you were good," Jill insisted. "But if you don't want to take it from me, I understand. I mean, what do *I* know? I've only been in the club for three years and watched hundreds of skaters try out."

Nikki laughed.

"Now are you going to stop moping and start look-ing forward to seeing me every day at practice for the rest of your life?" Jill said.

"Okay," Nikki said. "But will you do one favor for me?"

"Sure. Name it," Jill said.

"Cross your fingers for me—for good luck?" Nikki asked.

"You bet. I'll even cross my toes," Jill replied.

Tuesday after her last class Nikki was standing in the hallway at school, struggling with the lock on her gray metal locker. She could barely remember the combination—all she could think about was getting to the ice rink and finding out whether she had made Silver Blades. The new members' names were going to be posted that afternoon.

"Having a little lock trouble?" Kara called out cheerfully.

"Yeah," said Nikki, pounding the gray metal door with her fist. Suddenly it popped open. "I think the school gave me this locker just to torture me."

"It's just because everything's so old around here. Don't worry, you'll get the hang of it soon," Kara assured her, pushing her blond hair back from her face. Today she was wearing a sleek black jumpsuit. "Hey, you missed a great time at the mall Saturday. You should have seen the gorgeous guy working in the record store. Wendy and I hung out there forever, pretending we needed his help finding things."

"That sounds like fun," said Nikki. "Did you find any good music for the dance?" Nikki hoped the group hadn't done too much yet so she could still be involved.

"We got a couple of great CDs," Kara answered. "Didn't we, Jeff?" She turned to a good-looking boy with black wavy hair who had just come up behind her.

"Good stuff," he agreed. "I listened to them last night. Hey, Nikki. Kara said you're coming to the dance committee meeting Thursday."

"I sure am," said Nikki, suddenly feeling a little shy. She didn't know that Jeff even knew who she was. She only recognized him from seeing him with Kara.

"Jeff and I were just about to go to the first meeting of the school newspaper staff. I'm the new features editor," Kara said.

"Congratulations." Nikki smiled. "I used to be on the newspaper at my old school. We had a pretty decent paper."

"Why don't you come with us?" Jeff suggested. "I'm the editor-in-chief. I can find something fun for you to do."

"I can't today," Nikki said. "I have to go to the rink for skating practice." She didn't want to tell Kara and

Jeff how afraid she was that she wouldn't make Silver Blades.

Kara wrinkled her nose. "You never have time for anything but ice-skating. Come on, Nikki, this will be fun."

"Do you really skate every single day?" Jeff asked.

Nikki nodded, tucking a strand of hair behind her ear.

"That's great," Jeff said. "That's kind of how I am about basketball."

Suddenly Kara tugged on the sleeve of Nikki's sweater. "Don't look, but the hottest guy in school is right there—at the water fountain. Isn't he the cutest?" Kara whispered, continuing to glance down the hall.

"Here she goes again," Jeff said with a laugh.

"I can't tell," Nikki replied. "I can't get a good look at him." All she could see was the back of a tall boy with broad shoulders and long brown hair.

"Look again. He just turned around," Kara said. "But act casual."

Nikki slowly turned her head. Now she had a clear view of him. He was wearing a black T-shirt and faded jeans. "Who is he?" she asked Kara.

"Crush number two thousand and one," Jeff teased. "Or is it two thousand and two?"

Kara glared at Jeff, but she was smiling. "All I know is his name is Kyle Dorset, and he's in the eighth grade. He's new, like you, Nikki. Isn't he gorgeous?"

"I'm outta here," Jeff said. "See you at the newspaper office." He laughed, and headed down the hall to the newspaper office, shaking his head in disbelief. Nikki couldn't help smiling—Kara *was* being pretty silly.

She glanced at the new boy again. "You know what? I think that guy plays hockey at the ice rink where I skate."

"He does?" Kara asked.

Nikki nodded. "His friend bumped into me yesterday in the lobby of the rink, and both of them were wearing hockey gear. He must play in the hockey league."

Kara's blue eyes lit up. "Are you serious? I can't wait to tell Wendy and Jenny. This is great! You've got to meet him and tell me *everything* you find out. Promise?"

"I'll try," agreed Nikki. She had no idea when the Seneca Hills Hawks practiced or played their games. She didn't know if Kyle was even on the team. "Look, I have to go. My mother's waiting outside," Nikki said, grabbing the books she needed out of her locker.

"Don't forget to meet him!" Kara called as Nikki jogged down the hall toward the school's main doors.

Nikki burst through the doors into the afternoon sunshine and was startled to see Jill and Danielle standing at the bottom of the steps.

"Nikki!" Jill called out first. Nikki smiled and hurried over to them.

"What are you guys doing here?" Nikki asked. Nikki looked across the parking lot, where her mother was waiting in the car.

"We go to school here, remember?" Jill asked.

"I know *that*, but—"

"My mom's late, as usual. In fact, if you make the club, we should start a car pool," Danielle said, moving her backpack to her other shoulder. Her honey-colored hair was in a short braid, and a silver necklace hung around her neck. The necklace had a silver skate charm on the end of it.

"Wow! That's a beautiful necklace," Nikki said. "Where did you get it?"

"I have one too—see?" Jill fished the necklace out from under her red-and-black-striped mock turtleneck. "Danielle, Tori, and I all got them for each other last year. It's kind of like our own personal Silver Blades thing."

"For good luck," Danielle added.

"I need all the luck I can get today," Nikki said.

Jill held up both her hands, showing Nikki that all her fingers were crossed for luck. "My toes are crossed too—you just can't see them," she joked.

"Nikki, if you make the club, come find us right away, okay?" Danielle asked.

Nikki nodded. "I will." *If,* she thought. If I don't make Silver Blades, I don't know what I'll do.

"Can you see anything?" a little girl with blond hair asked, standing on tiptoe.

"Stop shoving!" cried a tall girl with dark red hair.

"Let me see!" demanded the boy behind her.

"Okay, kids, stop acting like animals. Everyone will get a chance to see the list," said Toby Mullen, the pro shop owner. Nikki had met him the first day she'd gone to the arena, when she'd bought new skate laces. Now Toby's head was sticking up above the crowd, and he was waving his arms around. "Let's try to form an orderly line. Come on, now. Line up."

Nobody paid attention to him. Kids were pushing and shoving as everyone tried to get to the bulletin board.

"Move out of the way!"

"I can't believe I didn't make it. Why didn't they pick me?"

Nikki squeezed through the crowd, ducking under someone's arm, then pushing her way past more kids.

Finally she stood right in front of the bulletin board. She could feel her palms sweating as she lifted her finger to the list to scan it for her name. On the left side was a column labeled "New Members." Underneath was a message written in large red letters: "New members please report to Mr. Weiler's office at 3:15 for a brief meeting."

Nikki skimmed the list. Paul Delaney . . . Gary Hernandez . . . Kelly O'Reilly . . . Christine Rosenblum . . . Sara Russell . . . There it was! Nikki Simon! She had made it!

Nikki whooped with delight and pushed back through the crowd to her mother. "Mom, I made it!" She wrapped her arms around her mother in a big hug.

"I knew you could do it," Mrs. Simon said, squeezing Nikki tightly.

"Thanks, Mom," Nikki said.

"Don't thank me!" Mrs. Simon protested, stepping back. "I didn't go out there and skate my heart out in front of those judges."

Nikki smiled. "I did, didn't I?" For the first time it hit her: She'd made the club by skating a terrific tryout.

"But thanks for moving here—for taking a chance on me," Nikki told her mother.

"Are you kidding? This is only the beginning." Mrs. Simon winked at Nikki. "You'd better get changed—practice starts soon, doesn't it?"

Nikki grinned as she took her duffel from her mother and ran down the hall to the locker room. Her mother was right. This *was* only the beginning—a great beginning.

5

"The first thing I would like to say is welcome to the club." Mr. Weiler smiled at the new group of seven skaters sitting on the floor of his office. There were two boys and five girls, including Nikki. "You should all feel proud to have been chosen. Over two hundred skaters tried out this year."

Nikki looked at a young girl sitting next to her and smiled. She still couldn't believe it. She was actually *in* Silver Blades. She was sitting in a room with *the* Franz Weiler.

"But I am afraid to tell you that the easy part is over," Mr. Weiler continued. "I am sure you have all heard that Silver Blades is a lot of work. The bad news is it's true."

The two boys, Gary Hernandez and Paul Delaney, laughed.

"We require many things of you. You will all practice every morning before school—some of you as early as five forty-five—and we will not put up with tardiness," Mr. Weiler said. "And you will return after
school at two every day for another three hours of
practice."

Nikki raised her hand. "How will we get out of school
so early?"

"Good question. Your schools will arrange your
schedules. You'll all be allowed to skip gym, since
you'll be getting more than enough exercise here,"
Mr. Weiler explained with a smile. "You'll take ballet
lessons—yes, even you." He looked at the boys. "And
weight training as well, for everyone."

"Even me?" Kelly O'Reilly, the small girl next to
Nikki, asked.

Mr. Weiler nodded. "Any skater needs to be strong,
even if she's only eight. Let me tell you a little about
our club. We now have twenty-six members, ranging
in ages from eight to fifteen. We compete often—as
often as possible. As you know, the goal of every
skater in this club is to make it to the level of national and international competitions. Perhaps some
of you know that several past Olympic competitors
have trained here. My goal as director of this club is
to get each and every one of you up to that level. Toward that end there is something I want to impress
upon you, before you go out to your first practice.
What we require more than anything in this club is

your complete dedication. You've been chosen to be a member. And that means you'll need to give skating all of your attention, every day. Skating takes precedence over everything else, from now on. Is that clear?"

Nikki nodded and saw everyone else in the room do the same.

"All right. That said, don't forget, you're doing this because you love skating. It's hard work, but you must enjoy it too. Because if you don't, it will show in your skating." Mr. Weiler stood up from behind his desk. "I expect to see you all on the ice in half an hour for your first group practice. But before then you should all stop by the pro shop and pick up a pair of Silver Blades warm-ups. Welcome!"

Nikki got up from the floor and smiled at Mr. Weiler. "Thank you for choosing me," she said nervously.

"Don't thank me yet," Mr. Weiler said. "Wait until after your first practice—oh, that reminds me. Each of you will be assigned to an individual coach in the next few days. Watch the bulletin board for details."

Nikki walked out of his office, chatting with Sara Russell and Christine Rosenblum on the way to the pro shop. She was so excited—now she would have a Silver Blades jacket just like Jill's. Mr. Weiler had made the club sound like it was going to be tougher than Olympic training camp. Well, if that was true, Nikki was more than ready. She'd been waiting for years for this chance!

She couldn't wait to call Katy, Erica, and Tom back home and tell them the good news.

Nikki was warming up on the rink fifteen minutes later when she spotted Tori Carsen. Tori was working on her spins in the far right corner of the rink. Nikki waved to Tori, and Tori smiled and waved back.

Nikki was about to go over and tell Tori she had made the club, but as she skated closer, she changed her mind.

"Do the sitspin one more time, and straighten that leg this time!" A woman with long blond hair was standing with her hands on her hips, screaming at Tori. The woman's raspy voice echoed throughout the cavernous rink. Nikki wondered who she was—maybe this was a new coach she hadn't heard of yet. If so, she hoped she wasn't always so angry and unpleasant.

When Tori didn't move right away, the woman wrapped her cashmere coat tighter around her body and shook her head. "Tori, you're the best skater in this club, but the only way you're going to stay that way is if you practice, practice, practice. I've raised you to be the best, but if you stop working, another skater will take your place. So do it again."

Nikki couldn't believe what she'd just heard. Not only was Tori's mom coaching her, but she was being incredibly harsh too. She couldn't remember ever see-ing such a high-pressure mom before. Her own mother was probably sitting in the snack bar drinking coffee and reading a book. Mrs. Simon had always left the instructing to Nikki's coach. Nikki couldn't imagine how it would feel to have your own mother yell at you about your skating. How did Tori stand it?

Nikki knew she should skate away and ignore them, but she couldn't help herself. She was transfixed. She skated in a small circle around the same little spot and continued to watch Tori.

Tori shook her blond curls and smoothed the flowing skirt of her light-blue skating dress. A row of sequins along the collar sparkled under the rink's fluorescent lights. I can't believe she's wearing such a fancy dress to practice in, Nikki thought with a twinge of jealousy. Her own best skating dress was nowhere near as beautiful as Tori's practice outfit, and she only wore that dress for special performances.

Tori began to circle the ice for her sitspin. Self-conscious about standing and staring, Nikki decided she should skate too. She also wanted to work on her sitspin.

Finding an empty patch of ice, Nikki created a circle by doing backward crossovers. Then she leaned and stepped with the outside edge of her left skate blade into the center of the circle. In one fluid motion Nikki whipped her right leg around while bending her left knee and squatting very low to the ground. Slowly she brought her head down and put her arms out gracefully in front of her outstretched leg, all the while concentrating on controlling the rapid spinning motion. She needed to complete thirteen revolutions for the sitspin to be considered correct. Then, keeping her weight on her left skate, she stood on one leg and pulled her right leg around rapidly. This motion made her right leg appear as if it were coiling around her left leg. Nikki ended triumphantly in the rapid spin known as the scratch spin.

"Tori!" Mrs. Carsen cried. Startled, Nikki quickly put both feet on the ice.

"Look at that new girl," Mrs. Carsen went on, loudly enough for Nikki to hear. "She's good, very good. If you don't keep up with our extra practices, that girl will show you up." Mrs. Carsen crossed her arms over her chest.

Nikki turned, curious to see which skater Mrs. Carsen was talking about. The other new female skaters were on the opposite side of the ice. Nikki's eyes opened wide with shock when she saw Tori's mother pointing directly at her!

"Congratulations!"

"What?" Nikki whirled around on her skates, totally disoriented.

"I said, congratulations! You know, as in hurrah, you made it!" Jill announced with a flourish, throwing her arms up in the air. Danielle was beside her.

Nikki grinned. "Thanks. I'm so psyched!"

"We told you you'd make it, didn't we?" Danielle added with a smile.

"I guess you guys *do* know what you're talking about," Nikki admitted. "Now all I have to do is—

Watch out!" she cried suddenly. An older girl with fiery red hair pulled into a tight bun shot past them and leaped into a double jump. The girl was so close, Nikki could feel the breeze she created as she went past her. She landed only a few feet away.

"That's Diana Mitchell. You've got to watch out for her, because she never watches out for *you*," Jill said, looking exasperated. "Diana jumps wherever and whenever she wants to."

Nikki stared at the red-haired girl in disbelief. Every skater knew it was her responsibility to watch out for other skaters before doing a jump nearby.

"Hey, there's Tori," Danielle said. "Does she know you made the club?"

"No . . . I mean, yes . . ." Nikki's face turned red. "I was going to go over and tell her, but . . . well, she seemed kind of busy with her mother. I didn't know her mother was coaching her."

Both girls nodded.

"Yeah. Poor Tori," Jill said, glancing across the rink. "Her mom isn't officially her coach—Mr. Weiler is. But her mom really pushes her."

"She never lets up," Danielle added softly.

"That must be hard for Tori," Nikki said. "How does Mrs. Carsen know so much about skating?"

Jill pushed her bangs out of her eyes. "Tori's mom used to be a really good figure skater herself a long time ago, but she never made it to the Nationals or anything."

"Sometimes I think Mrs. Carsen wants Tori to make

it even more than Tori herself does," Danielle added.

Nikki wanted to tell them what she'd overheard Mrs. Carsen saying earlier, but then changed her mind. She was still the new girl, and Tori was one of Danielle and Jill's best friends. Nikki saw Mrs. Carsen walk over to talk with Mr. Weiler, and a minute later Tori sped across the ice toward the three girls, spraying snow as she stopped in front of them.

"Hi, guys," Tori said. "What's up?"

"Nikki made the club," Jill announced. "Isn't that great?"

"I figured you must have. Congratulations," Tori said, smiling faintly at Nikki.

"Thanks," Nikki said. "That's a fantastic skating dress. I was admiring it before, when you were busy with your mom. I wish I had one that beautiful."

Jill shook her head. "Keep dreaming, Nikki. You'll never get an original Carsen skating dress. Mrs. Carsen only designs dresses for Tori."

"Tori's mom is a fashion designer," Danielle explained. "She has her own line of clothes, but they're really expensive."

"Really? Wow," Nikki said, impressed. "That's cool."

"I'll tell my mom you liked the dress," Tori said, skating in a small circle around the other three.

"Tori's mom thinks that if Tori looks the best, she'll get the best scores," Jill joked. "As if!"

Tori stuck out her tongue at Jill, who laughed. Tori stopped skating, and Nikki realized that Tori was looking her up and down, eyeing her pink sweatshirt and black leggings. Nikki blushed.

"It must be tough being new in town and in the skating club," Tori commented.

"It's not so bad," Nikki mumbled. "At least I've made some friends now." She smiled at everyone, flashing her braces. Tori was the only one who didn't return her smile.

"You know, skating with Silver Blades is a lot of hard work," Tori said in a serious tone.

"So I've heard," Nikki said. "Mr. Weiler gave us the lowdown earlier."

"You have to be ready for anything," Tori continued.

"Come on, Tori, the club isn't *that* bad," Danielle said. "I mean, we're all still in it, aren't we?"

"Yeah, if we survived basic training with Kathy, we can survive anything," Jill added.

"I don't mind hard work," Nikki said.

"Still, you'll need to put in hours and hours of practice each day," Tori said, "especially if you want to improve on that sitspin you did a few minutes ago."

"What was wrong with it?" Nikki asked.

Tori looked directly at Nikki. "It's just my opinion, but I think you need to work on your form. You look kind of awkward and amateurish when you spin."

"I don't think so," Jill said. "I think Nikki has a great sitspin."

Danielle didn't say anything, and Tori shrugged. "All I know is what I saw," Tori said. Then she turned

and skated back to the corner of the rink, where her
mother was waiting for her.

What's her problem? Nikki wondered as she
watched Tori go. Just a minute ago Nikki had been
feeling lucky because she'd made some fast friends.
Now it seemed as though she'd made an enemy too.

6

"**N**ikki, I'm going to work you hard, and I mean *work*. I have one rule that all my students must follow—you show me every last ounce of energy in everything we do in our lessons. If you're going to do something halfway, don't do it at all. Got that?" Kathy asked, her breath coming out in puffs in the cold air.

Except for Kathy's voice, the rink was eerily quiet. It was 5:45 A.M. on Thursday morning, and many of the Silver Blades skaters were still arriving. The overhead lights were dimmed, giving the ice a gray cast. Nikki nodded at her new coach. "I understand."

"Okay, then. Do that camel spin again. And use more power this time!" Kathy took her hands out of her pockets and reached for her thermos of steaming coffee.

Nikki performed the camel spin again, putting forth all her energy. She could feel that this spin had more power than the first one, and she smiled as she finished it.

"Why are you smiling?" Kathy frowned as Nikki skated over to her. "You looked like a dog at a fire hydrant! Straighten your leg and arch that back!"

Trembling, Nikki circled the ice again. No one had ever criticized her skating so harshly before. She swallowed hard and spun again, powerfully, with her back arched, and her leg so straight that her knee hurt.

Instead of congratulating her when she finished, all Kathy said was, "Change-foot sitspin. Go!"

After taking a few seconds to catch her breath, Nikki began to spin. A change-foot sitspin started out like a regular sitspin, but halfway through you had to change from spinning on your left foot to spinning on your right. You had to keep one leg out in front of you and stay in a sitting position the entire time. For the final rotations, you were supposed to change back to your original spinning foot. It was difficult not only to maintain balance but also to sustain enough power for all the rotations while changing feet.

As Nikki performed the spin, Kathy watched closely. "Again!" she yelled between sips of coffee. "And don't let me see your backside sticking up in the air this time."

Nikki could feel the perspiration forming on her brow. She skated over to the side and took off her new Silver Blades warm-up jacket and tossed it onto the bleachers. Underneath she was wearing a white T-shirt over black Lycra leggings.

Nikki was determined to get the change-foot sitspin right. After four more attempts Kathy finally nodded, but Nikki couldn't tell whether that meant Kathy was satisfied or that she just wanted to give up and move on.

"Let's see some jumps," Kathy said. "Do an axel first."

Okay, thought Nikki, now I'll show her. I know my axel is great. She stroked down the center of the rink. Other skaters, aware that she was having a lesson, moved out of her way. Nikki concentrated for a few seconds and then propelled herself high in the air on the outside edge of her left skate blade. Pulling her arms tightly into her chest for momentum, she made the one and a half turns counterclockwise and then landed cleanly on one foot. That was it! Nikki thought triumphantly.

"I told you at the beginning of the lesson that if you were not going to put all your energy into it, forget it. I don't know what you thought that jump was, but it wasn't an axel. Next time spring up—pop that takeoff," Kathy snapped.

Nikki stared down at the ice, afraid that if she looked at Kathy, she would burst into tears. For a second she thought about skating off the ice and never coming back. Then she reminded herself that Kathy was trying to make her better—even if she was being mean about it.

You came here to improve your skating, Nikki told herself. You knew it wouldn't be easy.

Nikki performed the axel again and again, until she was exhausted. She did layback spins and camel sitspins. Then she showed Kathy her double-toe loop. This was a jump involving a backward takeoff from the left toe pick and two full rotations in the air. After completing four of them, Nikki thought she might finally hear some praise from Kathy. Once again she was wrong.

"You barely got off the ground, Nikki. Show me some *power!*" Kathy yelled. Embarrassed, Nikki glanced around quickly, sure every skater on the rink had overheard. Surprisingly, no one seemed to notice that she was being humiliated by her new coach.

She couldn't believe the way Kathy was treating her. For the hundredth time that morning Nikki wished she were back in Missouri with her old coach, Eloise. Eloise was sweet and kind and had never yelled at Nikki, even when she was doing something wrong.

Nikki rounded the rink again. Then, facing backward, she dug her toe pick into the ice and with all her energy pulled her tired body up into the air. She spun around once, twice, but she didn't have enough height, and her body was tilted in the air. She came down too fast, barely landing on two feet. Nikki cringed and skated over to Kathy, ready to hear the worst.

Kathy only sighed and tucked a loose strand of her dark-blond hair back into her ponytail. "Enough for today," she said. Relieved, Nikki managed a weak smile. Every muscle and joint in her body was crying out in pain. "But, Nikki," Kathy continued sternly, "you're in the big leagues now. No more playing around. Every time we meet, I'm going to work you like I did today—and harder. If you want to skate like a top-ranked skater, you've got to start practicing like one. Okay?

"We have a lot of work to do in a very short time," Kathy went on. "There's a competition coming up in a couple of months, one that I'd like to see you enter— for experience more than anything else. But before you can be allowed to compete, you'll need to pass the United States Figure Skating Association test for that level."

"Okay," Nikki mumbled, looking up at her new coach. Things didn't sound completely hopeless. She had taken several USFSA tests before. These tests were a lot like the Silver Blades tryout. In order to qualify for national and international competitions, the skater was required to perform different jumps, spins, and footwork patterns perfectly in front of officials. If Nikki wanted to go to the Olympics someday, she'd be taking a lot of these tests in the coming years.

"The officials conducting the tests are flying out from USFSA headquarters in Colorado and will be here Saturday," Kathy informed her.

"*Next* Saturday?" Suddenly Nikki panicked. The test

for the next level included the double flip, the jump she'd fallen on while trying out for Silver Blades.

Kathy nodded. "I know we don't have much time," she said. "So you and I are going to have to work on that double flip nonstop until you can land it. And when I say nonstop, I mean practicing on the ice *and* off the ice. I mean going over the jump in your mind every minute of every day." Kathy placed both hands on Nikki's shoulders and said in a very serious tone, "Anybody can be a good skater, Nikki. But to be a great skater you have to give the sport total dedication and devotion. Think you can handle it?"

"I know I can," Nikki said, sounding more confident than she felt. She wanted Kathy to know how serious she was about her skating. Landing the double flip was one of the first steps toward the Olympics. Nikki wasn't going to let one jump stand between her and her dream. She'd pass that test next Saturday—and land that double flip—no matter what.

"What are we waiting for?" asked Nikki later that afternoon. She sat in the backseat of Mrs. Panati's four-door sedan alongside Jill and Danielle. Danielle had offered her a ride home.

"My pain-in-the-neck older brother, Nicholas," Danielle said.

"I didn't know you had a brother," Nikki said.

"If I were related to Nicholas, I wouldn't advertise it either," Jill joked. "Nicholas is only a year older than us, but he has this warped idea that he's so much cooler than we are."

A boy with spiky brown hair who closely resembled Danielle sauntered out of the arena's main doors. He didn't seem to care that everyone was waiting for him. He was carrying a large duffel bag.

"Hey, Mom." Nicholas stuck his head through the open window. "Can we drive my friend home? He needs a lift."

Mrs. Panati turned and looked in the backseat. "We don't really have room for another person."

"They can squish. He just made the team, and besides, I kind of already told him it was okay," Nicholas said.

At first all Nikki saw was another huge duffel bag coming through the front doors. Then she saw the boy's face following it.

"I can't believe it," Nikki whispered to Jill and Danielle as the two boys stowed their bags in the trunk. "That's Kyle Dorset, the guy Kara is nuts about."

"What guy *isn't* she crazy about?" Jill replied, turning around to get a better look at him.

"I promised Kara I'd find out more about him," Nikki whispered. "He's new in town."

"Here's your chance." Danielle giggled as the door opened and Kyle started to slide into the backseat beside Nikki. Nicholas climbed into the front.

There was a long silence as Mrs. Panati pulled out of the parking lot and onto the main road. Danielle introduced everybody, and then there was another silence. Nikki knew she had to say something to Kyle. This was probably the best chance she'd ever get, and she didn't want to blow it. She just wished he wasn't sitting so incredibly close to her—it made things even more awkward.

What would Kara want me to ask? Nikki wondered. She'd want to know if he had a girlfriend. I can't ask him that, she decided. I have to start with something less personal.

"So . . . um, are the Hawks a good team this year?" Nikki finally managed.

Kyle seemed as embarrassed as Nikki felt. He stared at his knees. "Yeah, we're okay," he said in a low voice. "We've only played a few games so far, though."

"Don't be so modest, man. Kyle just made the team, and he's already the top scorer," Nicholas told everyone.

Now we're getting somewhere, Nikki thought. Kara would love the fact that Kyle was really good at hockey. "Do you . . . play any other sports?" she asked Kyle.

"Sure. Basketball, football, soccer, baseball, tennis—"

"Is there anything you *don't* play?" Jill interrupted.

"Badminton," Kyle said, grinning at her.

Nicholas laughed. "Right. Actually Kyle holds the new record for SuperChase down at the arcade in the mall too."

Nikki smiled. "What kind of game is that?"

"You sit in a cockpit, like you're driving a race car," Kyle said. "Then there are all these road hazards you have to get around."

"I can't wait to get my driver's license," Nicholas commented. "That'll be so cool."

"*I* can wait," Mrs. Panati said. "Thank goodness that won't be for a few more years."

"Spare us," Danielle said. "Don't let him take the test, Mom."

"Uh . . . Mrs. Panati," said Kyle abruptly. "I live at the very end of this block."

Nikki shot Jill and Danielle a panicked look. Kyle was going to get out of the car in a minute, and he'd just started talking.

"I heard you just moved to Seneca Hills," Jill said quickly. "Do you like it here? Where are you from?"

"I lived in Colorado before this, and Michigan before that. My family moves around a lot," said Kyle. "My dad's in the Air Force."

"Nikki's new this year too," Jill said. Kyle glanced at Nikki as the car pulled up his driveway and stopped. He opened the door and practically fell out onto the pavement because he had been so jammed up against the door. Mrs. Panati popped open the trunk, and Kyle took out his duffel bag.

"Thanks. See you later, Nicholas," he called, walking up to his house. Mrs. Panati was backing out of the driveway when Nikki noticed Kyle had left one of his hockey gloves in the backseat.

"Mrs. Panati, stop!" Nikki said. She jumped out of the car and ran up the driveway. Kyle was just opening the front door, and he turned around.

"I think you dropped this," Nikki said, holding out the glove to him.

Kyle blushed as he took the glove. "Thanks," he muttered. "Thanks a lot."

"No problem," Nikki said. "See you!" She hurried back to the car. Kyle seemed like a really nice guy. She couldn't wait to tell Kara all that she'd found out about him!

7

"**H**ow's my favorite skater?" Mr. Simon greeted Nikki when she walked in the door ten minutes later.

"Exhausted." Nikki sank into a chair at the kitchen table. "You wouldn't believe how hard my new coach Kathy is. And I can't believe I've been up since five o'clock."

"Don't worry, you'll get used to the routine," Nikki's mother said. "Is Kathy really that demanding?"

Nikki groaned. "She doesn't think anything I do is good enough. And she says I have to land my double flip in the next ten days, or I won't be able to pass a test to get me up to the next level for a competition."

"That reminds me." Mrs. Simon grabbed a package off the counter. "This came for you today."

"It's the video I ordered!" Nikki said, excited. A few weeks ago she'd sent away for a skating video advertised in the back of a magazine. Now she ripped open the brown cardboard package and pulled out the tape called *Mastering Difficult Jumps.* "Wow, I completely forgot about this. This is just what I need!"

"How's that?" asked Mr. Simon.

"Just today Kathy was saying that I'd have to eat, sleep, and breathe the double flip if I wanted to land it," Nikki explained. "I'm sure it's on this tape. This has stretching exercises, pointers—everything. It'll be great."

"Maybe you should check it out with your coach," her mother suggested. "It might conflict with something she's trying to show you."

Nikki nodded. "You're right, Mom—I'd better show it to Kathy first. The last thing I want to do is make the 'Sarge' mad at me." Her parents laughed. Nikki stuck the tape in her skating bag and headed upstairs. She was about to change into her sweats when she remembered it was Thursday night. She was supposed to go to Kara's after dinner to help with the dance committee. Right now she was so tired, it was the last thing she wanted to do.

Nikki sighed. She had to go to Kara's. There was no way she could let her friend down again.

"Great, you're here!" cried Kara as Nikki walked into the rec room in the basement of Kara's house. "Hey, everyone, listen up. This is Nikki Simon," Kara announced. "She just moved in next door."

There was a chorus of hellos. "Hi," Nikki said, smiling at the group.

"This is Craig, Wendy, Jenny, David, and, well, you met Jeff the other day," Kara continued. "Have a seat, Nikki—help yourself to some food."

"I like your skirt," Wendy said when Nikki sat down next to her on the couch. "Did you get it around here?"

"Yeah, at that store Canady's, in the mall," Nikki answered, glancing down at her short flowered skirt. "Thanks."

"Canady's is a great store," Jenny said, nodding her approval. "They've got the coolest outfits there."

"Speaking of outfits," David said, "did you guys see Julie Jenson's mother when she came out of the house this morning?"

"See her? Who could miss her?" cried Craig, laughing. "You gotta love those big pink fuzzy slippers—"

"And that pink terry robe!" Wendy interrupted, giggling.

"At least it was better than yesterday's outfit. Remember that lime-green and yellow-striped thing she was wearing?" Kara asked.

"She looked like some weird kind of bug," Jenny said, laughing.

"Hey, Nikki, didn't you see Mrs. Jenson in that outrageous outfit this morning?" Jeff asked.

"No," Nikki said, stifling a yawn. "I don't take the bus in the morning. My mom drives me to school after my morning skating practice."

"Well, you missed a funny scene," Wendy said, playing with the hole in the knee of her well-worn jeans.

"Did you guys see last night's episode of *Hollywood High*?" Kara asked the group.

"*I* sure did. That new character, Kevin, is totally cute," Jenny commented. "I *was* getting sick of that show, but not anymore!"

"He looked like a dork to me," answered Craig, stuffing a brownie into his mouth.

"You'd think anyone was a dork if he wasn't a jock like you," Jenny teased him.

"What did you think of the new guy on the show?" Wendy asked Nikki.

"I don't know," Nikki admitted, embarrassed. "I watched *Hollywood High* all the time last season, but this year I've missed the first two episodes. I have to go to bed before it comes on so I can get up and skate really early." Nikki stared down at her hands folded on her lap. She felt really out of it sitting there, almost as if she lived on another planet. Not only was she incredibly tired, but her life was so different from everyone else's. Sometimes she wished she could sit around and watch *Hollywood High* too.

"Okay, enough small talk—the fall dance is less than a week and a half away, and we've got to get working," Kara said. "I think everyone should volunteer for a job. Wendy's made a list of all the things that need to happen."

Wendy took a piece of notebook paper out of her purse. "Okay," she began, flipping her long, strawberry-blond hair over her shoulders. "First we need someone to coordinate all the music and hire a deejay."

"I'll do that," David volunteered, stretching out his long legs as he leaned back in his chair. "I've got a great record collection with my older brother, and I also know the guy who runs the local radio station. Maybe I can get him to help out."

"That sounds great," Wendy said. Then she continued listing jobs—arranging for food, setting up the gym, and designing posters. After each one somebody volunteered, usually with great ideas. Nikki hadn't jumped in yet because she wasn't sure she was going to have time for any of them—they all sounded like a lot of work. She was already struggling a little to balance her new Silver Blades schedule with schoolwork.

"And lastly," Wendy said, "we need someone to take care of buying and making decorations and contacting the balloon company for the helium-filled balloons."

"I'll do it," Kara volunteered.

"I can help too," Nikki said. Maybe if she worked with Kara, she'd be able to contribute enough time.

"Okay, we're all set!" Wendy said. "Now, get to work—well, tomorrow anyway."

Kara turned to Nikki. "This is going to be so much

fun!" she said. "Let's go shopping for decorations right after school tomorrow."

"Tomorrow isn't great for me because of skating," Nikki said. "But I'll definitely find time in a couple of days—maybe this weekend."

"Okay," Kara said, shrugging. "Whenever."

Nikki glanced around the room, making sure no one would overhear her.

"Guess what?" she whispered. "I talked to Kyle after practice today."

"You're kidding!" Kara said. "Why didn't you call me when you got home?"

"I haven't had any time. My new schedule is pretty tight," Nikki explained. "I have practice first thing every morning at five forty-five—"

"Five forty-five A.M.? Are you crazy?" Wendy asked, joining them.

Kara was eager to hear the details. "So, what happened? What did Kyle say?" she asked.

Nikki briefly recounted the story of the car ride home from the rink, making it sound a little more exciting than it had actually been. "He's a really nice guy," she concluded.

"I knew it! I'm in love!" Kara cried when Nikki finished her story. "What else do you know? Where does he hang out? I barely see him around school."

"That's basically all I know," Nikki said. "But if you can't find him at school, you should try the ice rink. He's there a lot of the time."

"Thanks, Nikki—this is *great*," Kara said, grinning.

Nikki smiled. She hadn't done anything all that incredible, but at least Kara had forgiven her for not being able to shop for decorations tomorrow.

"Is this me or what?" asked Nikki, holding up a gold Lycra skirt and a silver sequined top. She spun around the clothing store Saturday afternoon in the mall, pretending to waltz.

"Don't you think it's a little early for Halloween?" Jill laughed.

"It's not *that* bad," said Nikki. Then she took another glance at the shiny material. "It's worse than bad," she admitted with a giggle. "Tori, you have such great taste in clothes. Can you help me find an outfit for our school dance?"

"Sure," Tori said eagerly. "How about something on this rack over here?" Nikki, Jill, and Danielle followed Tori across the store.

When Jill had called that morning, inviting Nikki to go to the mall with the three of them after practice, Nikki had been wary of spending time with Tori. Since the episode earlier in the week, she and Tori had been keeping a polite distance from each other at the rink. But now Nikki was glad she'd come. She really liked Tori. She was funny, and she did have great taste.

Tori held up outfit after outfit, all of which were either not Nikki's taste or too expensive. "Let's get out of here," Nikki suggested after a few minutes. "I should probably be looking for decorations for the dance anyway."

"Why?" Danielle asked, picking up an animal-print scarf.

"That's my job on the dance committee. You guys should join the committee too. The first meeting was a lot of fun," Nikki said.

"It probably was fun," said Jill, holding up a pair of long silver earrings to her ears. "But you'll learn. We all did."

"Learn what?" Nikki asked as the four girls left the store.

"Silver Blades is really intense, and then there's homework. There's no time for anything else," said Danielle.

"I'm used to doing a lot of things at once," Nikki said. "In Missouri I was on the paper and I organized all kinds of school activities. My skating won't suffer."

"I'm sure Nikki can handle it. Besides, it's not good to spend all your time skating," Tori said.

Jill gave Tori a baffled look. "What? You never do anything else."

"I know, but some people need to be well-rounded," Tori said. "Maybe that's what Nikki wants to do."

"Hey, let's grab a slice of pizza," Danielle said, interrupting the conversation as they approached the food court.

The others quickly agreed.

Nikki was glad the subject had been dropped. She

knew she could handle being on the dance committee even if Jill and Danielle didn't agree. At least Tori seemed to think it was a good idea.

The four girls each ordered a slice and then carried them to a nearby table. Nikki stared in amazement as Jill dumped hot-pepper flakes all over her slice.

"It needs flavor!" Jill said, catching Nikki's gaze.

"So how are your lessons with Kathy going?" Danielle asked Nikki before popping a sliver of pepperoni into her mouth.

"Okay," Nikki asked. "Only, she's incredibly tough on me."

"Maybe Kathy isn't the best choice for you," Tori commented.

"Why not?" Nikki asked, surprised. "She's supposed to be one of the best coaches in the country—isn't she?"

Tori nodded. "That's true," she acknowledged. "But she's very demanding, and not everyone can take it. Maybe you're one of those people."

Nikki carefully watched Tori wipe the corner of her mouth with a napkin. What did she mean, "one of those people"? It sounded as if Tori was calling Nikki a wimp. Suddenly Nikki wished she'd never come to the mall with Tori. Was Tori so competitive that she was going to try to scare Nikki out of Silver Blades?

If she thinks she's going to scare me off, she's wrong, Nikki said to herself as she angrily bit into the slice of pizza. I don't give up that easily!

"You're *not* going to believe who's here," Jill said as she skated in a circle around Nikki. Both girls were working on their spins, using up the last few minutes of early-morning practice time Monday morning.

"It's Kathy and the double-toe loop police," Nikki said, grinning. "They've come to take me away, right?"

"Good one!" Jill said, hitting her playfully on the arm. "Now you know why everyone calls Kathy the 'Sarge.'"

Nikki rubbed her thigh muscles. "Do I ever. Does she torture everyone?"

"Pretty much," Jill said. "But you'll get used to it. Anyway, Kara, Jenny, and Wendy are standing over there by the boards."

"You're kidding!" Nikki couldn't believe Kara was at the rink on a Monday morning at seven, before school started. What was she doing here?

Nikki skated over to the girls and stopped abruptly in front of them, spraying ice shavings from her blades. "What's up?" she said.

Jenny looked impressed. "I love how you stop that way," she said. "Every time I try that, I end up wiping out."

"Usually in front of a bunch of cute seniors," Wendy added with a yawn.

Nikki laughed and looked at Kara, who seemed very

tired—and annoyed. "We rode our bikes all the way down here at the crack of dawn, and he's not even here," Kara complained.

"Who's not here?" asked Nikki, confused.

"Kyle," said Kara. "Remember you told me if I wanted to see him, I should come to the rink? I knew you had practice every morning, so I figured he did too. I thought I'd come to the rink and pretend to be visiting you, but really I'd be watching Kyle," she explained.

"The hockey league usually practices *after* school," Nikki explained.

"Great," Wendy grumbled. "I got up at six-thirty just to come with Kara."

"Sorry," Nikki apologized. "I didn't think you guys would actually come to the rink so soon. If you'd asked me, I would have told you more about when he practices."

"I thought it would be fun to surprise you," Kara said. "I guess it was a stupid plan." She looked extremely disappointed, and Nikki felt guilty that her friend had come all this way for nothing.

"I'll introduce you guys another time—I promise," Nikki said eagerly. "How about if you casually drop by this afternoon around five o'clock?"

"I've got an even better idea," Kara declared. "The next time you see him at the rink, will you do me a really big favor?"

"Sure, what?" Nikki asked.

"Ask him if he's going to the dance. I need to know if he has a date yet. If he doesn't, then I'll ask him," Kara said. "Okay, Nikki?"

"That's a great idea," Jenny agreed.

Nikki wasn't so sure. She didn't want to ask Kyle lots of questions again. She felt stupid—and what if she wound up ruining the whole thing for Kara?

"Please?" Kara begged. "I'd do it for you."

Nikki shrugged. "Okay. But after I find out if he has a date, you're on your own!"

8

"**N**ikki, before I forget, here's that videotape you wanted me to look at," Kathy said, handing the tape back to Nikki at Tuesday morning's early practice. "The exercises look good—you can go ahead and do them on your own time."

Nikki smiled, glad Kathy approved of the tape. She quickly skated to the side and tucked the tape in her skating bag.

"Let's get right to work on that double flip," Kathy said. "Give it all you've got."

Nikki adjusted her gloves and skated around her end of the rink, preparing to jump. Up in the air Nikki rotated twice and came down on two feet—as usual. She threw up her arms in frustration. She could feel how close she was to landing the jump, but so far she hadn't been able to manage coming down on one foot.

Kathy waved her over. "You're still not getting up high enough in the air. As a result you don't have enough time to complete both rotations fully and you end up landing on two feet. Follow me," Kathy commanded, skating toward the far end of the rink.

The coach stopped under a rope that spanned the narrow part of the rink. The rope looked like a clothesline and hung about twelve feet in the air. Attached to the middle of the rope was a metal wheel with another loose rope hanging from both sides. Kathy skated over to the side and reached behind the boards. She pulled out a heavy, wide leather belt with hooks attached to it. Bewildered, Nikki stared as Kathy brought the belt back to where Nikki was standing, under the middle of the rope.

"What's that?" asked Nikki.

"This contraption is a teaching device for jumping," Kathy said. "That round metal circle is a wheel called a pulley. Now first we strap you into this vest, which is called a harness."

Kathy loosened the buckles and fit the wide leather strap around Nikki's waist. Kathy pulled it tight and buckled it up. The belt wasn't uncomfortable, but Nikki felt ridiculous, as if she were about to perform a circus trick.

"Next we hook you to this pulley," Kathy explained, reaching for the vertical rope hanging off the pulley.

Nikki felt a tug on her lower back as the hooks were fastened together.

Kathy swiftly skated around Nikki and grabbed the other end of the rope that was attached to the pulley. "Here we go," she announced.

"What am I supposed to do?" Nikki asked. She felt as if she were strapped in to go skydiving.

"Ignore the harness," Kathy said, "and do your double flip."

Nikki skated backward a bit. The rope that was hooked to the harness on one end and held by Kathy on the other end was fairly long. Nikki found she had plenty of room to skate.

Turning, and digging her toe pick into the ice, Nikki launched into the air. Suddenly she felt a sharp tug on her back where the harness was hooked to the rope. She pulled her arms in and rotated around. Turning seemed to be easier than ever before, and Nikki completed two revolutions. As she came down, she could feel the taut pull on the rope loosening. She landed shakily on one foot.

"Wow! I landed it—sort of. I still don't understand how this works, though," Nikki said.

"A quick explanation and then back to work. As you jump up, I pull down on this end of the rope that I'm holding. By my pulling down, the wheel of the pulley turns, moving the rope with it, and hoisting you into the air. The pulley only gives you a few extra seconds to be suspended in the air. But that's enough time for you to become accustomed to the proper arm and leg positions and learn how to land the jump," Kathy said in a very businesslike manner. "Now let's see that double flip again."

Nikki jumped high in the air, pulling her arms close to her chest. She turned twice and was able to land on one foot. This thing is great! she thought, repeating the jump.

As Nikki worked, Kathy called out some occasional instructions, such as "Higher!" "Arms in!" and "Bend those knees!"

"Enough of this," Kathy said after about ten more minutes. She unbuckled Nikki from the harness and put it away. "Do the double flip on your own now. Remember to position your body the exact way it was in the harness."

Confident, Nikki skated in a small circle. She had landed the jump at least a dozen times in the harness. She threw herself into the air. Managing to rotate only once, Nikki fell onto her rear end.

"What was that?" Kathy called to her. "Come on— remember what you just learned and use it!"

Brushing the wet ice shavings from her skirt, Nikki prepared to jump again, trying to recall the feeling she had had while in the harness. She leaped up into the air again, this time keeping her body still. She was able to complete both rotations, and her right foot touched down on the ice for the landing. She wobbled on her blade a little, but she kept her balance.

"Great!" cried Kathy. She actually sounded a little

excited. "Next time don't be so wimpy. Land solidly!"

Nikki was so thrilled, she felt like yelling, but she knew Kathy wouldn't approve. She had finally landed the jump correctly! She thought once she did it, she'd be able to keep doing it—but the next time she landed on both feet. The third time she landed on her right foot, but she fell.

"That's enough for today!" Kathy called out after several more failed attempts. "It's getting there," Kathy commented as Nikki skated over to her. "Keep practicing. I mean total-concentration practicing. Every time you're on the ice, you should be jumping, and at home work on the jump in front of a mirror and start using that videotape you showed me."

Nikki nodded. She had only a few more days to practice before the test. If she was going to pass it, she didn't have any time to waste.

Later that afternoon Nikki's mother dropped Nikki off at the rink. Nikki quickly changed into her practice dress and laced up her skates. The snack bar and the rink were fairly quiet. Most of the figure skaters and the hockey players were just beginning to arrive.

Nikki hurried over to the corner table of the snack bar, where Danielle was reading a textbook. Tori was sitting next to her, flipping through a magazine.

"Hi. Where's Jill?" Nikki asked, dropping down into a plastic orange chair beside Danielle.

"She should be here any minute. She had to go home and watch her little brothers while her mother took her little sister to the dentist. It's crazy how much she has to baby-sit for those kids," Tori said, still flipping through the magazine.

Nikki nodded, then decided to go buy some juice. She still felt uncomfortable around Tori. She never knew whether the other girl was going to be sweet or mean to her. Today Tori seemed to be in a good mood.

"Look who's here," Danielle whispered to Nikki as she stood.

Nikki watched as Kyle walked into the snack bar with Bobby Rodgers. Bobby was a member of Silver Blades, but he was in the ninth grade, and Nikki didn't know him very well yet.

"Aren't you supposed to ask Kyle to the dance for Kara?" Danielle asked.

"All I'm going to do is ask if he has a date. If he doesn't, Kara is going to ask him to the dance *herself*," Nikki said. She still couldn't believe she had agreed to do this for Kara.

"Hi, guys," Bobby said. He and Kyle were standing in front of their table. "Can we sit here?"

"Of course," Tori answered sweetly, pulling out the chair next to her. Bobby sat there, and Kyle took the empty seat next to Nikki.

Nikki chewed her lower lip as she sat back down. She had no idea how she was going to bring up the dance.

"How's it going?" Kyle asked Nikki as he bit into a

chocolate-chip cookie. "Are you getting used to Seneca Hills?"

"It's going really well," she told him, smiling. "Silver Blades is great, and I like school a lot too. Actually I've gotten involved in some interesting projects there."

Interesting projects? Nikki repeated in her head. I sound like I'm talking about a science fair, not a dance.

But Kyle didn't seem put off by her dull-sounding comment. "That's great," he said. "What kind of things are you involved with?"

Nikki nervously tapped her fingers on the table. "I'm on the fall dance committee," she began. "My friend Kara Logan is the head of the committee. Kara's great. With Kara in charge the dance will probably be the best in the history of Grandview Middle School."

"So what kind of things are you doing for the dance?" Kyle asked.

Nikki could see Danielle grinning over the top of her textbook. Kyle had totally missed all her references to Kara. What was she supposed to do now?

"I'm doing the decorations—with Kara, of course. She's so much fun. Do you know her?" Nikki asked. She was sure he would understand what she was getting at now, unless he was completely dense.

Kyle shook his head. "No, I don't." He took a sip of soda. "Don't you guys have to be here for practice all the time? How can you do stuff at school too?" he asked.

"Well, it's hard, but I manage," Nikki said. "Actually, Kara's done most of the work so far. She really loves to dance. What about you guys?" she asked desperately. "Do you like to dance?"

"Yeah, it's a real blast," Bobby muttered in a sarcastic tone. He shot Kyle a glance that seemed to say, What are we doing wasting time with these silly seventh-graders?

"I'm not a very good dancer. I guess I need someone to teach me," Kyle said, glancing at Nikki. Danielle raised her eyebrows, but Nikki ignored her.

"My friend Kara's a fantastic dancer," Nikki went on. Then, unable to wait any longer for Kyle to catch on, she blurted out, "Are you going to the school dance on Saturday?"

"Why, are *you*?" Kyle quickly replied.

"Um . . . yeah, I guess so," Nikki replied. She was trying to think of a way to ask if he was going by himself when Bobby stood up and pushed back his chair.

"Come on, Kyle, let's go. You said you'd show me how to play that new video game." He pointed to the machines at the back of the snack bar.

"Sure," Kyle said. He stood up and turned to go. "See you guys later," he said. Then he smiled at Nikki before following Bobby to the video game.

"Great," Nikki moaned after Kyle and Bobby had left. "I still don't know if he's going to the dance with anyone, and I couldn't even get him to *ask* me about Kara."

"I don't think Kyle cares who *Kara* is," Tori commented.

"I don't get it. Kara's the most popular girl in the seventh grade. How could he not care?" Nikki asked.

"Did it ever occur to you that Kyle's not interested in Kara because he's more interested in *you*?" Danielle suggested.

"You should have seen the way he looks at you," Tori added. She opened her eyes extra wide and gazed at Nikki with a lovesick expression. Danielle burst out laughing.

Nikki blushed. "You guys are totally imagining things. It's just that he didn't understand that I was trying to get him to talk about *Kara*—that's all."

"Right," Danielle said.

"Well, I've had enough of playing matchmaker," Nikki said. "Kara can deal with Kyle herself from now on. I have my own problems—like my double flip—to work on."

Tori's expression changed abruptly. "Have you been working on it a lot?"

"Nonstop," Nikki admitted. "I think all my other jumps and spins are ready for that USFSA test, but I just can't get the double flip. I landed it once this morning."

"You're kidding," Tori said. She didn't sound excited.

"No, I landed it—once. Every time after that I fell. I'm doing everything I can to learn it too," Nikki said.

"Really? What kinds of things?" Tori asked.

"Working with the harness and spending every minute I can on the ice practicing," Nikki answered. "And

I'm going to start using this tape." Nikki pulled the black plastic videocassette case from her skating bag. "I ordered it—the tape shows lots of different exercises and movements to do to help land double jumps. It's great."

"If the tape's so great, why can't you land the jump more than once?" Tori challenged.

"I just got the tape in the mail last week," she replied shortly. "And I wanted to make sure that Kathy thought it was okay."

"Oh," Tori mumbled, looking away.

Nikki hesitated. She knew Tori was working on her jump, too, and even though Tori was very competitive at times, Nikki truly did like her.

"Want to watch the tape with me?" Nikki offered. "Jill told me you're working on your double flip too."

"No, thanks. Do you really think I need a stupid videotape to help my skating?" Tori said. She stood and headed out of the snack bar without saying good-bye to Danielle or Nikki.

"What's Tori's problem?" Nikki stated out loud. "Why does she always snap at me like that?"

"Don't take it personally. Lately Tori's been very moody when it comes to skating," Danielle said.

"Why?" asked Nikki. "It seems like all I have to do is mention skating and she gets angry."

"I bet her mother has been pressuring her about the testing this week," Danielle said.

"So? That doesn't mean she should take it out on *me*," Nikki said angrily. She crumpled up her empty cup and tossed it into the trash can. There was only one thing to do: ignore Tori's competitiveness and practice until she knew she could land that double flip.

"Look, I'll see you on the ice," she told Danielle as she rose to leave.

"Nikki," Danielle said, playing with the zipper on her warm-up jacket. "Um . . . good luck. And don't let Tori get to you."

"Thanks," Nikki said. Don't worry, I won't! she thought, feeling more determined than ever.

9

Wednesday afternoon at two o'clock Nikki stood along the side of the rink and did some stretches. Then she quickly completed her warm-up on the ice. She'd changed quickly so that she could have some time alone on the ice before practice began.

Double flip. Double flip. The words ran through her mind as she worked on simple single-rotation jumps, building to more difficult ones. This afternoon the rink was fairly crowded with skaters. Diana Mitchell, the girl with red hair, kept practicing spins and jumps dangerously close to Nikki. Finally Nikki decided to move out of the way, and she skated over to an empty patch of ice. Tori and her mom were working nearby.

"I'm trying, Mom! Do you think I'm doing this on purpose?" Tori snapped.

"Frankly, Tori, I'm not sure," Mrs. Carsen replied.

"It looks to me like you don't really care about being eligible for the competition that's coming up."

Tori whirled around to face her mother, her face flushed with anger. "I *do* care, Mom. The problem is, you're always on my back. If you'd give me a break, I could learn the double flip." At that she skated away.

Nikki watched as Tori pushed around the ice, dug her toe pick in, and lifted into her double flip. But Nikki could see Tori's positioning in the air was a little crooked, and she wobbled the landing, touching down with two feet instead of one.

She's having the same trouble I am, Nikki realized. Tori skated in a tiny circle, working on her edges. She was wearing a sleek hot-pink unitard trimmed in electric blue. As usual, it was much nicer than anyone else's practice clothes. Nikki wondered whether Tori's mother told her what to wear, as well as how to skate. No wonder Tori seemed so competitive all the time.

Nikki forced herself to turn away from Tori and her mother and work on her own skating. Silently she repeated the words "Focus. Focus." She tried to remember how her body had felt when she was in the harness. Then, using all the energy she had, Nikki attempted the jump at least half a dozen more times, but she couldn't land any one of the double flips perfectly. She either fell or landed on two feet. She simply wasn't getting enough height.

One more time, Nikki said to herself. This time I'll do it. Holding her breath, Nikki dug her toe pick into the ice and threw her body high into the air. She didn't see Tori coming from the other direction, launching into her own jump, until it was too late.

Both girls came down from their double flips at high speeds, and they fell, crashing into each other. Tori screamed as the blade of Nikki's skate hit the back of her leg. Horrified, Nikki turned to look.

Tori was staring at the back of her leg, where a trickle of blood was seeping slowly through the leg of her pink unitard. She looked at Nikki.

"Tori, are you all right?" Mrs. Carsen called across the rink.

"I can't believe you, Nikki," Tori snapped. "Don't you look where you're going? You sliced my leg! I'm bleeding!"

Several other skaters rushed over and formed a circle around the two girls.

"I'm so sorry! Are you okay?" Nikki asked.

"Oh, no, Tori. Are you hurt?" Danielle cried.

"I'm sorry. I didn't see you. I'm sorry," Nikki repeated in a trembling voice.

Mr. Weiler pushed through the crowd. "What is going on here?" he demanded.

"I'm hurt. *She* sliced my leg with her skate blade." Tori pointed at Nikki. "And she did it deliberately too."

"I didn't," Nikki protested. "Honestly, I'm sorry, Tori!" Nikki felt guilty, but she also knew the collision was as much Tori's fault as her own. It was up to every skater to spot out where she expected to land and to look out for other people.

Mr. Weiler bent down and inspected Tori's leg. "Calm down, Tori. This is only a minor surface wound. It's already stopped bleeding. The front desk has a first-aid kit. Go out there, and they'll put a Band-Aid on it. There's no need to create a scene." He looked sternly at both skaters. "You girls must pay attention to where you're landing. This is how serious accidents happen."

He stood up and started to skate off, expecting Tori to follow him. But Tori remained on the ice, glaring up at Nikki. "I know you did this on purpose. You *wanted* to hurt me!" Then, before Nikki could say another word, she stood up and skated off the ice.

Nikki stood by the pay phone in the lobby of the ice rink, clutching a quarter, her heart still beating rapidly from the difficult practice. She'd skipped out a few minutes early, and she hoped her mother was home. If she could leave now, before everyone finished practice, she wouldn't have to face any of the Silver Blades members.

She still couldn't believe that Tori had publicly accused her of intending to hurt her. It wasn't true, but no one else knew that, and Nikki was sure that most of the skaters would believe Tori over her. They'd known Tori for a long time, and they'd only known Nikki for a week and a half.

She was about to slide the quarter into the coin

slot when she heard someone say, "Where have you been?" Jill and Danielle walked toward Nikki. "We've been looking all over for you."

"I . . . had to tell my mother something," Nikki lied softly.

There was a look of concern on Jill's face. "We thought you might be upset about what happened with Tori," she said.

Nikki's eyes filled with tears. "I wasn't trying to hurt her, you know. It was an accident."

"Of course it was!" Jill said. "Tori overreacts sometimes. She's under a lot of pressure from her mom because of the USFSA test, and she said a lot of things I'm sure she didn't mean. She'll forget the whole thing by tomorrow. Right, Dani?"

Nikki wasn't so sure. And when Danielle didn't reply right away, that confirmed it for her. Tori would never forget what happened on the ice today.

"So what did you need to tell your mom?" Jill asked.

"Actually I wanted her to pick me up. I figured you guys wouldn't want to car-pool with me today."

Danielle shook her head. "Nikki, we don't think you're a horrible person because you bumped into Tori. But . . . you should be more careful, you know."

"Come on, Dani," Jill said. "That stuff happens all the time. It was as much Tori's fault as it was Nikki's."

Nikki nodded. "I feel bad about what happened, but Tori should have been watching out too. I think we were both concentrating so hard, we were oblivious to anyone else."

"Right," Jill agreed. She looked at Nikki solemnly. "You'd better call your mom," she said.

Nikki stared at her, confused. Hadn't they just said they weren't mad at her?

"You need to ask her if you can have dinner at my house tonight," Jill continued with a smile. "Because there's no way you're going to land that double flip without some of my mom's spicy barbecued ribs."

Nikki grinned. "How spicy?"

"Let's just say you'll need a pitcher of ice water—for yourself," Danielle said as they walked toward the locker room. "Maybe two."

"Nikki, can I talk to you for a minute?" Kathy called out as the girls opened the locker-room door.

Uh-oh, Nikki thought. Here comes my lecture on not bumping into other skaters. "Sure, what is it?"

"I've been watching you and Tori work on your double flips all afternoon, and it occurs to me that you could each stand an extra practice session," Kathy said. "Why don't you come in half an hour earlier tomorrow morning—that'll give us some extra time with the rink to ourselves."

"Okay," Nikki said. She really did feel as if she was in basic training—that meant showing up at the rink at five-fifteen!

"When you see Tori in there, can you tell her that Mr. Weiler wants to start earlier too?" asked Kathy. "I need to run. I'm having people over for dinner and— well, never mind about that. I'll see you tomorrow at five-fifteen."

"Sure," Nikki said, nodding. "See you tomorrow morning." She walked into the locker room, where almost everyone had finished changing already. She didn't see Tori anywhere.

"Come on, Simon, let's go!" Jill urged. "I'm dying for you to see my house and meet all my brothers and sisters."

"I'm dying for those ribs," Nikki said. "I can't believe how hungry I am. Is Tori still here?" She stood on a bench and looked around the locker room.

"No, she left already," Danielle said. "Why?"

"If you're still worried about what happened earlier, don't be," Jill said.

"No, it's not that—I have to give her a message," Nikki said. "I'll call her tonight when I get home."

"Then hurry up and get changed," Jill said, "or my younger brothers are going to eat all the ribs before we get there!"

"Okay, okay." Nikki laughed. "You're as bad as Kathy, you know that?"

10

As soon as Nikki got home from Jill's, she headed upstairs to her room. She had homework to do, and she really wanted to watch the training video at least once before bed.

She was rewinding the tape to watch the double-flip section again when her father poked his head into the family room. "Why don't you call it a night, sweetheart—you must be exhausted."

Nikki was about to protest when she realized that she did feel tired, and tomorrow would be another early day. "Okay," she agreed.

"I'm really proud of your dedication," her father said, "but I'm worried about you. Mom and I want you to have fun too—are you sure that being a member of Silver Blades is what you really want?"

Nikki squeezed his hand, grateful that her parents were nothing like Mrs. Carsen. "Thanks, Dad. I really like Silver Blades—even if it is a lot of hard work."

"Okay, Niks," he answered. "Now, get some sleep!"

"You sound like the Sarge, Dad," Nikki said with a grin.

"That tough, huh?"

Nikki hesitated for a second. "Nah," she replied finally. "Not even close!"

Nikki hit the snooze button on her alarm clock for the third time. She just needed a few more minutes of sleep. Suddenly there was a loud knock on her door. "Nikki, Nikki, are you up?" her mother asked.

Nikki opened one eye and looked at the clock. "Mom, it's not even five o'clock."

Mrs. Simon opened the door. "You're supposed to be at the rink early today, remember?"

Nikki sat bolt upright in bed. The early practice! She had completely forgotten!

"We need to leave in the next few minutes if we want to get there by five-fifteen," Mrs. Simon said. "I'll go make a breakfast you can eat in the car."

Nikki hopped out of bed and rushed to her closet. She pulled out a clean set of practice clothes and quickly changed into them. She was so tired, she felt as if she were moving in slow motion. She stood staring into her bureau drawer, trying to choose which sweatshirt to wear, for what felt like five minutes. By the time she made it downstairs, it was already after five-fifteen.

"Kathy's going to kill me," she said to her mother as they got into the car a few minutes later.

"I'm sure she'll understand," said Mrs. Simon.

Nikki shook her head. "You don't know Kathy. She set aside this extra session just for us—oh, no! I forgot to call Tori to tell her to be at the rink early! They're *both* going to kill me."

Mrs. Simon patted her daughter on the leg. "Don't worry so much, Nikki. There's nothing you can do until you get there."

When Nikki rushed into the rink a few minutes later, she glanced up at the large clock at the far end. It was twenty minutes to six. She saw Kathy and Mr. Weiler sitting on the coaches' bench. She sat down to lace her skates.

As soon as her skates were on securely, Nikki skated over to where Kathy, wrapped in her navy-blue parka and holding her thermos of steaming coffee, was waiting. Mr. Weiler was sitting next to Kathy, and neither of them looked pleased.

"You're late," Kathy observed in a cold voice.

"Sorry," Nikki said.

As she did, she heard another voice behind her say, "I am?"

Nikki whirled around and saw Tori standing behind her.

"We won't stand for tardiness from either of you.

To be a great skater, one needs discipline." Mr. Weiler clapped his big leather gloves together as he spoke.

"But—it's not even five forty-five yet," Tori protested.

"You were supposed to be here at five-fifteen," Kathy said. "Didn't Nikki tell you?"

Tori folded her arms across her chest and stared at Nikki. "No, she *didn't* tell me."

"Tori's right," Nikki said nervously. "I forgot to tell her about starting early today. I didn't see her last night, and then—"

"There's no point explaining now," Mr. Weiler said. "We need to get on the ice and make the most of what little time is left. I understand this was an oversight, Nikki. But in the future we would appreciate it if our time was not wasted."

"I'm sorry," said Nikki. "It's all my fault. Tori, I—"

"I don't want to hear your excuse this time," Tori said. "Don't bother."

"Come on, Tori, I have half an hour left before my next lesson," Mr. Weiler said. "Get on the ice, and let's see what we can do." He skated to the opposite end of the rink.

Before Tori followed him, she turned to Nikki. "You know how important it is that I land that jump before the USFSA test on Saturday. How could you do this?"

"I'm sorry. It was a mistake," Nikki said. "A big mistake. I didn't mean to make you miss the session!"

"Do you really expect me to believe that?" Tori cried. "You'll do anything to hurt my chances of passing this test, won't you? Now I have only half an hour to work on my double flip. If I don't pass that test, I'll never forgive you," she said, staring at Nikki. "Never."

A few minutes later Nikki started working with Kathy as Mr. Weiler began his lesson with Tori. Nikki didn't have to look up. She knew Tori was watching her skate. Ignore her, Nikki told herself.

Nikki was building speed to try her double flip when she heard Mr. Weiler yell, "Yes! Tori, that's it! Perfect double flip!"

Nikki stopped to look at Tori, down at the other end of the rink. She was smiling, and Mr. Weiler was patting her on the shoulder.

"Nikki, your work is at this end of the rink," Kathy said sternly. "I shouldn't have to remind you."

Nikki nodded and started working on her preparation for the double flip. If Tori can do it, so can I, she thought. I did it once before.

Nikki tried to get her landing right on the double flip for the remainder of the session, but she kept messing it up one way or another. At one point she noticed Tori standing on the ice watching her as Mr. Weiler talked to another club member. She was sure Tori could hear all of Kathy's criticisms.

Tori's probably loving this, Nikki thought, wishing she could just melt into the ice beneath her. Despite what she'd told her dad about Silver Blades just last night, Nikki wished she'd never heard of the stupid skating club.

On Thursday at lunch Kara, Wendy, and Jenny gathered around Nikki to hear about her conversation with Kyle in the snack bar. Nikki was so exhausted, she could barely remember what had happened. She told them how many times she had brought up Kara's name, deciding not to mention Tori and Danielle's opinion that Kyle wasn't interested in Kara. Nikki had enough problems right now. "So now all you have to do is ask him to the dance yourself," Nikki told Kara. "I don't think I can do anything else."

"I don't know if I'm ready to talk to him yet," Kara said. "He's so shy and he keeps to himself so much—"

"But, Kara, you talk to everybody," Nikki argued. "You're the least-shy person I know!"

"I guess . . . but when it comes to some guys, I don't know—I just freeze up and sound really dumb," Kara said. "I can't ask Kyle out."

"Just think about how guys ask us out." Wendy punched Kara in the arm. "Hey, want to go to the dance with me?" she said in a low voice. She and Jenny started laughing.

Kara shook her head. She did not look amused. "Listen, Nikki. I'll make a deal with you. You promised the dance committee you'd help me make the decorations. But all week you haven't had any time to go to the mall with me to shop for materials. You were also supposed to call the helium-balloon company and find out if they could supply the balloons."

"Oh, Kara," Nikki told her, blushing. "I'm really sorry I haven't called them yet. By the time I get home from skating practice each night, the balloon company is closed."

"That's okay. Here's my offer. I'll take care of the balloon company and I'll pick up all the supplies for the decorations. The only thing you still have to do is make the paper chains *and* find a way to ask Kyle to the dance for me. That would be perfect."

"How can I do that?" Nikki asked her.

"I trust you," said Kara. "Don't worry—you'll think of something."

Nikki felt as though she didn't have a choice—Kara was helping her a lot with the decorations. She owed her. "All right," she told her friend.

Hockey pucks slammed against the boards as Nikki walked into the Seneca Hills Hawks practice on Thursday afternoon. All the players were on the ice, working on passing drills, and each person was covered in padded hockey gear. Nikki couldn't tell one player from the next. Kyle had to be out there somewhere.

She walked over toward the bleachers on the side of the rink, hoping no one would notice her. Finally she spotted Kyle's green-and-gray parka thrown over one of the lower bleacher benches. Every time she had seen Kyle, he was wearing the same distinctive jacket.

She pulled the note she had written for Kara out from the top of her skate. She'd decided that the best way to handle this was to sneak a note into Kyle's jacket pocket so she wouldn't have to tell him in person that Kara liked him and wanted to go to the dance with him. It would be a lot easier this way, Nikki reasoned. He'd find the note after practice, and then he could talk to Kara directly, without Nikki's being involved. Nikki unfolded the note and read it once again:

> *Dear Kyle,*
>
> *I would really like to go to the fall dance this Saturday with you. I know you said you're not a good dancer, but I could help you learn. I think you're great.*
>
> *From a hockey fan who also happens to be the president of the dance committee*

Nikki tucked the note into Kyle's pocket, then turned and quickly scanned the rink. For a second she thought she saw someone looking in her direction, but all the boys had their helmets on, and it was hard to tell them apart.

She hurried out of the rink toward the weight room, glad that planting the note had been so easy. Now all Kyle had to do was ask Kara out—and get the whole thing over with!

"Ouch." Nikki strained to lift her legs. She squeezed her eyes shut and held her breath. She pushed and pushed. Nothing happened. The weight wouldn't budge.

"Feel free to give me a hand here anytime," Nikki said to Ernie Harper, the Silver Blades weight trainer.

Ernie chuckled. "That wouldn't be fair," he said as Nikki relaxed her leg muscles and stopped trying to lift the weight. "That was a strength test, since it's your first session with me. Something tells me you've never worked out before."

"How weak am I?" asked Nikki.

"Let's just say that when it comes to strength, you're closer to a tick than a Terminator."

"But at least I'm a tick who can ice-skate," Nikki joked.

Ernie laughed. He was a small but powerful-looking, muscular man with curly dark hair. "Once the other girls get here, we'll start," he said.

Now that Nikki was working out, she was feeling a little better. Somehow the activity was lifting her spirits and making her feel more hopeful about her skating. She'd land that double flip yet.

Nikki also felt relieved this was a group training session. She had never used equipment like this before.
All she had done at her old rink were sit-ups and
push-ups. Sitting on the seat of a Nautilus machine
in the far corner of the room, she watched Ernie adjust
the amount of weight on a machine that looked like a
torture device she had seen in an old movie.

Suddenly Jill, Danielle, and Tori burst into the room.
Sara Russell and Hillary Ford were behind them. Tori
was walking on her toes, and her arms were poised
stiffly above her head. Her lips were pursed tightly, and
in an exaggerated French accent, she said, *"Balance.
Jeté. Arabesque developpé. Ze arabesque*—it should be
grande. Ah, Mis Danielle. Ze Madame, she iz vedi vedi
upset wit your arabesque."

Danielle giggled as Tori pranced about the room,
her cheeks sucked in, her nose up in the air.

"I am Madame, ze best ballerina in France!" Tori
cried.

"Stop. You're making me laugh so hard, my stomach
hurts!" Jill exclaimed.

"Tori's doing an impression of this substitute teacher we had in ballet class the other day," Danielle
explained. "You guys will get to meet her next week
when you start lessons. Our regular teacher's in Russia
for a month."

"Tori imitates her perfectly," Jill said. "This woman
is a prima donna who thinks she's France's gift to
ballet. Right, Tori?"

Tori nodded, without looking in Nikki's direction.

Nikki smiled stiffly. "That was funny." She couldn't think of anything else to say. She'd just about given up on ever being friends with Tori. "You sounded very French, anyway."

"I doubt you would know," Tori said coldly, half under her breath, but loud enough for Nikki to hear.

"Listen, Tori, I apologized this morning," Nikki said heatedly. "I don't know how many times I can tell you I'm sorry—but I am sorry I forgot."

"Did you really forget?" asked Tori.

"What do you mean?" Nikki demanded.

"I mean, it seems pretty convenient that you forget to tell me about a special practice session that's going to teach me how to land the jump *you* can't do," Tori said, sitting on an exercise mat across the room.

"But I thought you did the double flip on Tuesday," Danielle said to Nikki.

"I did," Nikki said.

"And *you* landed it this morning, right?" Jill asked Tori.

Tori nodded. "No thanks to her."

"So what's the problem?" Jill went on, ignoring Tori's comment. "It sounds to me as if you're both almost ready for the test. I bet you'll both be able to land the jump."

"Maybe," Tori said. "But I lost my chance to get an extra half hour of practice in this morning." She glared at Nikki. "If you ask me, someone's trying to sabotage me."

"Come on, Tori—you've been watching too many old movies," Danielle said. "No one's out to get you. We're all in this together."

"That's right," said Jill. "Nikki told us she wanted to tell you about the practice yesterday, but then I dragged her off to my house, and I'm sure she just forgot."

Nikki was grateful for Jill and Danielle's support. "That's what happened," she said to Tori.

"Fine," Tori said. Nikki could see that nothing they had said had made an impression on her. Tori's mind was obviously made up.

A piercing blast from a whistle made all six girls turn to the front of the weight room, where Ernie was standing. "Enough talking, girls. Time to start pumping iron," he said.

Nikki breathed a sigh of relief. It's time to forget about Tori Carsen! she told herself. If the other skater didn't want to be reasonable, there was nothing Nikki could do or say to make her.

11

At the rink early Friday afternoon Nikki furiously pulled out the contents of her locker. One glove. Two gloves. Hairbands. The rag she used to clean her skate blades. An extra pair of rubber skate guards. After she had thrown every single item in her skating bag onto the locker-room bench, Nikki groaned loudly. "Where is that dumb videotape?" she cried.

Nikki had planned to watch the video and do the exercises last night. But she hadn't been able to find the video anywhere.

Now she searched her skating bag again. She dumped all the books out of her backpack. No tape.

"Have you seen a videotape in a black box?" Nikki questioned every girl in the locker room. Nobody had.

Panicked, Nikki ran out of the locker room in her stocking feet. She jogged down to the far end of the hall and into the snack bar, where she searched under every table and chair. She asked the woman behind the counter. She asked a couple of hockey players eating hamburgers. No one had seen her videotape.

Nikki hurried out of the snack bar and opened the door to the weight room.

"Nikki, what's wrong?" Ernie asked. He was supervising two boys who were doing push-ups.

"Have you seen a training videotape in a black plastic box?" she asked breathlessly. "I lost it."

"Nope, sorry. I'll keep an eye out for it, though," said Ernie.

"Thanks!" Nikki called, already out the door. She took a step down the hallway and entered the pro shop. A little bell rang when she opened the door. Toby stood behind the glass counter up front. He was talking to Kathy and Mr. Weiler.

"Nikki," Toby said, adjusting the baseball cap he wore over his straight brown hair. "What can I do for you?"

"I'm looking for a videotape," Nikki explained quickly. She turned toward Kathy and asked, "You don't happen to have it, do you?"

"I gave it back to you earlier this week," Kathy reminded her.

"I don't understand where it could be," Nikki wailed. "I've been carrying it around in my skating bag, but when I looked for it last night, the tape wasn't there."

"Maybe it fell out of your skating bag at school?" Toby suggested.

Kathy and Mr. Weiler were wrapped up in their conversation and didn't offer any other suggestions. Nikki wanted to cry. She had been sure that this tape was going to help her land her double flip for tomorrow's test. But now, when she needed it most, it was missing. Exasperated, Nikki ran out the door and back toward the rinks.

Jill and Danielle were standing in the hallway talking to Danielle's brother, Nicholas.

"What's the hurry?" Jill asked as Nikki hurried over to them. "You have the same look on your face that Randi gets when there's no more peanut butter left for lunch."

"I'm looking for my videotape—you know, the one I told you guys about on Tuesday? I can't find it, and I've been searching everywhere!" Nikki told the group.

But nobody had seen it. "It's just so weird," Nikki said. "I hardly ever misplace things. Do you guys think you could help me look?"

"Of course," Danielle said, putting her arm around Nikki's shoulder. "I'll ask all the skaters in the rink."

"Why don't we check the locker room again," Jill suggested. "I'll help you retrace your steps."

Nikki sighed with relief as she turned toward the locker room with Jill. At least she had someone to help her. They were passing the boys' locker room when the door opened and Kyle dashed out. When he saw Nikki, his face turned pink.

"Hi, Nikki," he said. "Listen, I'm late for a scrimmage, but I got your note."

"But that wasn't—"

"If you're still interested, I'll go to the dance with you," he mumbled.

"But—"

"I have to go," he called over his shoulder. "See you later." He disappeared inside the hockey rink.

Great, Nikki thought. This is just great. Now what was she going to do? And what was she going to tell Kara?

"What was that all about?" Jill asked. "Does he have a crush on you or what?"

"I left a note for him that was supposed to be from Kara. Only he thinks it was from me! He must have seen me." Nikki groaned. "Kara's going to hate me."

"Doubtful," Jill said. "Don't worry about Kara's love life—you have more important things to deal with."

"Like finding that tape before practice starts," Nikki agreed.

Nikki glided toward the center of the rink, weaving her way past the other skaters. The practice session was almost over, and Nikki was relieved. She was ready to go home. She had searched with Jill and Danielle for the videotape for over half an hour with no luck. She didn't want to risk bumping into Kyle again either.

She had tried to do the double flip for a full fifteen minutes, but each time she'd either double-footed the landing or wobbled on the ice on her right skate. She was growing less and less hopeful about landing the jump in the USFSA test. She wasn't usually a quitter, but she just couldn't get a handle on the jump.

Nikki decided to concentrate on perfecting her flying camel spin for the last few minutes of the session. She could see Kathy glaring at her from the music booth as she put some new music on the sound system. Nikki knew she would get a speech from Kathy about not practicing the double flip every waking moment, but she just couldn't concentrate.

The flying camel was similar to a camel spin—the only difference was the approach to the spin. With the flying camel, Nikki had to perform a high-flying leap onto her spinning leg. Using the momentum from the jump to propel the spin, Nikki raised one leg arabesque-style. As she picked up speed, Nikki concentrated on centering the spin and keeping up the speed.

Not satisfied with her approach into the spin, Nikki practiced the first leap several times. She worked on the transition from the jump into the spin, controlling the pace on the jump so that the spin began smoothly. It felt great to lose herself in her skating. Ten minutes later she stopped to catch her breath. The Zamboni, the tractorlike machine that cleaned the ice, was driving onto the rink. Most of the skaters had already left.

Nikki got off the rink, sat on the bleachers, and took off her skates. As she slipped on her sneakers, she looked around for Jill or Danielle. They weren't in the rink. She figured they were already outside waiting for Danielle's mother.

Nikki grabbed her skating bag and hurried into the locker room. She had to change in a hurry. Nikki was pulling her sweater over her head when she heard Tori talking as she entered the room.

"You guys are not going to believe this," Tori was saying. "I was in the back of the pro shop before, trying on warm-ups, and I overheard Kathy and Mr. Weiler talking. Want to know what they said?"

"Sure," Danielle said.

"Of course—I love gossip," Jill agreed.

"You promise not to repeat any of this?" Tori asked solemnly.

"Naturally. Now, get on with the dirt!" Jill urged.

Nikki heard the girls walk to the other side of the locker room, down another row of lockers. She was about to announce herself when she heard Tori say, "Well, Kathy was talking to Mr. Weiler about *Nikki*. Kathy told him that she has never had a more hopeless skater than Nikki. She thinks Nikki's going to bomb out and embarrass them in front of the USFSA official tomorrow. And get this—she told Mr. Weiler that they made a *big* mistake letting Nikki into the club!"

Nikki put her hand over her mouth to suppress a gasp. Kathy had said all that—about her?

"That can't be true, Tori," Danielle protested.

"You must have heard wrong," Jill insisted. "We've all seen Nikki skate—she's excellent! They must have been talking about someone else."

"No, it's all true," Tori insisted. "I heard it word for word. I have to admit, I never thought Nikki's skating was quite up to our level. I always thought it was kind of ridiculous that she got into the club, and obviously Kathy agrees. But you can't say anything to *anyone* about this—especially not Nikki!"

Nikki grabbed her bag, turned, and ran out of the locker room. She didn't need to hear any more. It was all painfully obvious now why Tori didn't want to practice with her, or skate with her—she thought Nikki's skating was a joke. Tori didn't feel competitive at all! Nikki wasn't someone to compete with—she was someone to feel sorry for, and laugh at. Tori had been so mean to her because she thought Nikki's skating was bringing down the club, and she was probably trying to get her to quit.

Nikki continued running until she was outside the rink and down the street a few blocks. She was shaking all over, trying not to cry, as thoughts rushed through her mind. So that's why Kathy had been so harsh to her in practice. Nikki's getting into the club was a fluke, and now everyone was sorry she had made it.

They're right, Nikki thought. I'm not good enough for this club. I was crazy to think I could be a top skater. Forget about going to the Olympics someday. I'm so bad, they're embarrassed to have me in Silver Blades!

Then Nikki couldn't restrain herself any longer. She collapsed onto the curb, put her face in her hands, and started to sob.

For most of Friday night Nikki lay on her bed, doing nothing but staring at the little yellow and blue flowers in the wallpaper. She planned to spend the rest of the weekend the same way. She wasn't going to take the USFSA test. And she was never going back to the rink. She couldn't face Jill, Danielle, Tori, or Kathy after what she had just found out about her skating.

It's over, she thought, tracing the outline of a flower design on the comforter on her bed. It's all over. I'll never be a great skater. I'll never be anything but plain old Nikki Simon.

Sighing, Nikki glanced around her bedroom, letting her gaze fall on the pictures of skaters taped to her closet door. She felt like tearing them all down.

What am I going to do? She moaned and rolled over onto her stomach. I've been humiliated. Why did we ever have to come to Seneca Hills? Why couldn't we just have stayed in Missouri?

Nikki looked at the pictures of Katy, Erica, and Tom on her wall. Then she stared at the framed photo of Eloise hanging over her bed. She had always been so encouraging to Nikki, telling her she was special, she had talent. How could Eloise have misled her this way? Nikki wondered.

Nikki stared at the phone on the night table beside her bed, then sat up and picked up the receiver. She punched in the coach's telephone number. The phone rang three times on the other end. Then there was a click, and Nikki heard, "Hello, you have reached the home of Eloise Borden. I can't take your call right now. Please leave a message at the beep, and I'll get back to you as soon as I can."

Nikki waited for the beep. "Hi, Eloise. It's Nikki— Nikki Simon. I need to talk to you about Silver Blades. Can you call me back—please? You know the number. Thanks. Bye."

Nikki slowly replaced the receiver and flopped back down on her bed.

The phone on her night table rang suddenly. Nikki stared at it for a second. Could it be Eloise calling back so soon? "Hello?" she said.

"Nikki, this is Kara. How's it going?"

"Rotten," Nikki said, sitting up on her bed.

"Why? What happened?" asked Kara.

"Oh, I just . . . had a bad day at the rink," Nikki said, not wanting to go into it.

"Well, just forget about skating and think about how great the dance is going to be tomorrow night," Kara said cheerfully.

Nikki steeled herself, anticipating Kara's next question to be about Kyle. But to her surprise Kara asked about something else.

"Have you finished making the paper chains yet? We're going to meet at the gym at three tomorrow to decorate it."

Nikki stared at a stack of construction paper sitting on the floor in the corner of her room. She'd been so preoccupied with her skating the past few days that she'd completely forgotten about making the decorations.

"Uh . . . I'm not quite finished with them yet," Nikki replied hastily.

"What do you mean, 'not quite'?" Kara asked.

"Don't worry, I'll finish them in time," Nikki told her. She wasn't going to let Kara down again. If she had to spend all night gluing construction paper together, she would. It wasn't as if she had anything *else* to do tomorrow, anyway.

Nikki said a quick good-bye and hung up the receiver. Then she grabbed a pair of scissors from her desk, knelt down on the carpet, and began to cut sheets of paper into narrow strips.

A few minutes later there was a knock on her door. "Come in, Mom," she said in a bored voice.

The door swung open, and Jill walked into the room. "Surprise!"

Danielle followed Jill into Nikki's bedroom. "Hi," she said.

Nikki continued cutting construction paper into strips. She couldn't look at them.

"Where were you after practice?" Jill asked, sounding genuinely upset.

Nikki took a deep breath. "I overheard Tori talking to you guys this afternoon in the locker room," she slowly admitted.

"You *did?*" Danielle asked.

Nikki nodded. "I know that Kathy thinks I'm a horrible skater and that Tori agrees with her. I'm an embarrassment to Silver Blades. But don't worry—I'm going to drop out."

"Don't say that," Jill said.

"Why not?" Nikki retorted, finally looking up. "I'm wasting everyone's time. I can't believe it took me this long to figure it out." She shook her head. "All I ever wanted to do was to ice-skate, ever since I was six years old. My parents believed in my skating so much that they moved to Seneca Hills because of me. What a joke!"

"Nikki, don't be stupid!" Danielle suddenly cried, surprising both Jill and Nikki. "You're just giving up, like you don't care about skating at all. *I* know you care. And you're too good to give up!"

"I'm *not* good. Kathy thinks I don't work hard enough," Nikki argued. "She's told me so in my lessons. Obviously now she's telling everyone else I'm untalented too."

"Wait a second," Jill interrupted. "I don't know why Kathy was saying that about you today, but I do know that she yells. A lot."

"But she's *always* yelling at me," Nikki muttered.

"At me too!" Jill answered. "That's just her way. If she didn't care about you, she wouldn't even bother to criticize you. She yells in order to push her skaters. To help them. To make them tougher."

"My old coach, Eloise, was never mean to me. I skated fine with her," Nikki replied.

"But you've already gotten better with Kathy—admit it. And you'll continue to get better with her yelling at you," insisted Jill. "Better than you ever would have gotten with a sweet coach like Eloise."

Nikki didn't reply. She gave Jill a skeptical look. "Then why did Kathy tell Mr. Weiler that I was so terrible?" she asked. "If I'm as bad as Tori heard them say I was, why did they even let me into the club? Just so they could kick me out—and humiliate me?"

Jill shrugged. "Maybe Tori didn't hear them right."

"I think they were talking about someone else," Danielle chimed in. "Tori said she was in the *back* of the pro shop, trying on warm-ups. So how did she catch every word?"

"So—do you guys think I'm good enough to be in the club?" asked Nikki.

"Definitely," Danielle said. "You're one of the better skaters there."

"Tori doesn't think so," Nikki said. "I don't know— it's weird. I used to feel as if she thought I was good—

as if she was competing with me all the time."

"She *has* been competing with you," Jill insisted. "You're a big threat to her—and to her mom."

"You know what?" Danielle asked. "This is starting to remind me of an old movie I saw. There's this guy who plays football, see, and he—"

"Spare us and get to the point," Jill said, and Nikki smiled. Just watching Jill and Danielle tease each other was helping to cheer her up.

"This is going to sound mean, but—maybe Tori's trying to get you to drop out so she won't have to compete with you," Danielle said.

Nikki nodded. "The possibility has crossed my mind," she confessed.

"Look, promise us that you're not dropping out of Silver Blades," Jill said.

"At least until the USFSA test tomorrow," added Danielle. "I think you can pass it, and so does Jill."

"Yeah, and you should trust me," Jill joked. "I already took it, didn't I? And if I can pass it, you can."

Nikki managed a weak smile. "Thanks for the pep talk. I'll think about what you guys said."

Danielle was looking at the strips of construction paper on the carpet. "What are you doing?" she asked. "You're not still doing decorations for the dance, are you? I thought Kara was taking care of them."

"She is—except for the paper chains," Nikki said. "Did Jill tell you what happened with Kyle?"

Danielle nodded. "You're lucky—he's cute," she said with a grin.

"No, I'm not! Kara's going to kill me," Nikki said.

"So when do you need to have these paper chains finished?" Jill asked. She sat on the floor and picked up the scissors. "By tomorrow?"

Nikki nodded. "At three."

Danielle sat down next to Jill and picked up the bottle of glue. "Then we'd better get started."

"Are you serious? You'll help me?" Nikki asked.

"Of course, if *you* want to make them all . . ." Jill put down the scissors.

"No!" Nikki cried. "Please stay. And—thanks. For coming over to talk to me and stuff."

"No problem," Jill said.

"Hey, Nikki, do you have any cookies? I need to eat if I'm going to make a mile-long paper chain," Danielle said.

"I'll go get some snacks," Nikki said. "It's the least I can do."

Jill and Danielle left at about ten, and Nikki started getting ready for bed. She still hadn't decided what to do about tomorrow's test when the phone rang. Her mom picked it up downstairs, then called, "Nikki! Phone for you!" a few minutes later.

"Hello, Nikki, it's me," Eloise said warmly. "How are you?"

"Hi, Eloise!" Nikki replied. "Thanks so much for

calling back. I'm so confused." The whole story tumbled out.

"You're not serious about quitting, are you?" Eloise asked. "Nikki, you've never given up on anything before."

"I know," Nikki said. "It's just—I guess it's a lot harder than I pictured. Kathy works me so hard and never says anything positive."

"Kathy may be tough, Nikki, but she's also an excellent coach. Your mother told me that she already has you landing your double flip!" Eloise said.

"Yeah," Nikki admitted. "That's true. But I don't know what to do about Tori either."

"You can't change what people think of you, Nikki," Eloise replied. "All you can do is concentrate on yourself and on doing your best. Unfortunately, if you want to compete on the national and international levels, you're going to run into people who are highly competitive. You're going to have to learn how to handle it. It's a part of your training."

Nikki sighed. "Maybe I'm just not good enough."

"Listen to me," Eloise interrupted. "I *know* you're good enough. And I think you owe it to yourself to take the test tomorrow."

"You sound like my friends," Nikki said. "That's what they think too. I'm just not sure of what *I* want to do."

"It's your choice," Eloise said in a softer tone, "and it's your life. Remember that, and then please let me know what you decide."

"I will," Nikki promised. "Thanks for calling me back. I miss you, Eloise. Bye."

"I miss you, too, Nikki," Eloise replied. "Good luck."

Nikki hung up the phone and climbed into bed, lost in her own thoughts. It had felt good to hear Eloise's voice and her reassurances that Nikki was a good skater. *If only I could believe it myself,* Nikki thought.

As she reached over to shut the light, the latest issue of *Skating* caught her eye. There was a photo of Tonya Harding on the cover, in a pure-white skating dress. Tonya was smiling confidently.

"I used to think I'd be like her," Nikki grumbled to herself. She glanced around her room. Everywhere she looked in her room, she saw something related to skating: trophies, warm-up clothes, posters, her skating bag, a clump of brightly colored laces on her desk.

Abruptly tears welled in Nikki's eyes. *They're right,* she realized. *My friends and Eloise are absolutely right. I've worked so hard. I can't just walk away from skating—even if one of the best coaches in the country doesn't think I have any talent.*

She sat up in bed, thinking for a few more minutes, and then, her decision made, she shut the light.

Nikki was the first skater on the ice Saturday morning. She had dragged her mother out of bed extra early, because she wanted to make sure she had the maximum amount of time to practice before the test at noon.

The rink was quiet. Very few lights were on, and shadows covered the ice. As Nikki finished her warm-up with a high loop jump, the scraping sound of her skates echoed in the empty arena. Out of the corner of her eye Nikki noticed another skater stepping onto the ice.

It was Tori, dressed in a white skating dress with sheer white sleeves. She barely glanced at Nikki as she began her warm-up. What's she doing here? Nikki thought. She must have had the same idea I did.

For about ten minutes Nikki stayed on one half of

119

the rink and Tori stayed on the other. It was almost as if there were an imaginary line drawn across the rink. Neither she nor Tori said a word to the other or crossed the invisible line.

Nikki decided that she wasn't going to watch Tori. She had to concentrate on her own skating. She wasn't going to let Tori distract her or get her upset.

Nikki skated in a small circle on her side of the rink. She decided to start practicing her jumps with an axel, something she knew she did well. Facing forward, she raised her left foot slightly off the ground. With her weight on her right foot, Nikki took off on a forward edge and sprang up in the air. Nikki pulled her left leg around, which brought her high into the air. She landed solidly on one foot, after rotating one and a half times.

I'm jumping well today, Nikki thought. Then she glanced over at Tori. She couldn't help herself. Nikki was surprised to see Tori lift up into an axel too. Tori's axel was fast, her arms were pulled in tightly, and she landed cleanly. Tori then skated over to her mother, who was sitting by the side.

As Mrs. Carsen talked to her daughter, she pointed across the ice, directly at Nikki. For once she was speaking in a low voice, and Nikki couldn't hear what she was saying. She was glad. She wasn't going to get caught up in their little competition today. She turned her back to them and powered across the width of the rink.

Halfway across the ice, preparing for a split jump,

Nikki did a quick turn so that she was facing backward. She dug into the ice with her right toe pick and shot up into the air with incredible power. Spreading her legs straight apart in a split position, Nikki reached out and touched her toes with her fingertips. As she landed on one foot, a big smile crossed her face.

Nikki continued to skate around her side of the rink. Once again she couldn't resist glancing over at Tori. Tori powered across the rink, her blond curly hair bouncing on her shoulders with each stroke. Then Tori lifted into a marvelous high-flying split jump.

She's imitating me, Nikki realized. Tori's trying to prove she can do everything better than I can.

Nikki turned her back on Tori. Let her play whatever silly game she wants, she thought.

Finally it was time to attempt the double flip. Nikki visualized the jump, remembering how it had felt to be in the harness. She skated faster and faster, until everything became a blur. Her body felt loose and weightless.

Nikki whirled around and dug her toe pick into the ice. With all her strength, she sprang high into the air, pulled her arms in tightly, and began her rotations. One. Two. Before she knew what was happening, she had touched ground again—on one foot!

"I did it!" cried Nikki, throwing her fist in the air. All that work, all those harsh comments from Kathy— it had all been worth it! She glanced over at Tori. Tori didn't seem to want to imitate her any longer— she didn't attempt the jump right away.

Once isn't good enough, Nikki told herself. I need to be able to land that jump whenever the testing official asks me to. She practiced the double flip several more times, each time focusing on getting up high enough in the air. Her success rate was about fifty-fifty; for each time she made it, she fell once too.

Nikki stopped to take a short break. She was wiping her face with a towel when she heard a toe pick sharply hit the ice in front of her. She looked up just as Tori lifted straight up into the air. She watched, holding her breath, as Tori finished her two rotations, then touched down on one foot. She wobbled only slightly and held her finish.

Tori glanced at Nikki and smiled, looking happy for the first time Nikki could remember.

"Congratulations," Nikki said.

"Same to you," Tori said, just as applause started to sound in the arena. Nikki looked up at the bleachers and was surprised to see both Jill and Danielle standing and cheering.

Mrs. Carsen yelled, "All right, Tori! Way to go!"

Jill and Danielle pulled off their rubber skate guards and hurried onto the ice. Kathy Bart was suddenly in the rink, too, and she motioned to Nikki and Tori to meet her in the center of the ice. Nikki skated over and was caught in a hug first by Jill and then by Danielle. Tori was hugged by both friends too.

"I knew you guys would start landing that jump solidly sooner or later," Kathy said. "I'm glad it was sooner—I came down here early, hoping to see you both practicing it. I think that if you both concentrate, you'll be able to do it for the test. You've got the mechanics down cold."

Nikki smiled faintly at Tori. Maybe now that Tori had been praised, she'd stop treating Nikki like such an enemy. She wasn't going to count on it, though. She turned to skate away when she heard Tori's voice.

"Wait a second, Nikki—I have something to say," Tori suddenly announced.

Everyone turned to stare at her.

"I lied. I lied to you guys, but most of all, I lied to Nikki. And I'm really sorry," Tori said. She glanced nervously at Nikki.

"I don't understand," said Nikki.

"I knew you were listening to us talk in the locker room. I saw you go in, and I made Jill and Danielle come in with me afterward. I made up that story about Kathy saying you were a bad skater because I knew it would upset you," Tori admitted.

Nikki stared at the other skater. "You made it up?" she echoed.

Kathy frowned. "Tori. This is way out of line."

Tori studied her skates for a moment. "I was trying to get back at you, Nikki. When you bumped into me and then you forgot to tell me about the extra practice session Thursday—well, I thought you did it on purpose."

"I didn't!" said Nikki. "I felt terrible about that."

"I know that now," said Tori. "But there's something else." She paused. "Everyone always used to tell me that I was the most promising skater in the club—until you came along. Jill kept talking about you, and Kathy showed a lot of interest. Suddenly you were the favorite. I couldn't help it—I felt like I needed to show you that you weren't as great as everyone said." Tori glanced around the rink. When she saw her mother was still in the bleachers, she continued in a trembling voice, "My mother has been comparing me to you constantly. I'm never good enough for her. She wants me to be the best one in the club. . . . I guess that's why I took your videotape out of your skating bag too."

"Wow," Nikki said softly. "So that's where it went."

Kathy's eyes widened, but she didn't say anything.

"When I told my mother about it being a special tape to help you land jumps, she insisted on seeing it," Tori explained.

"I offered to share it with you," muttered Nikki. "Why did you have to steal it?"

"I don't know. I'm sorry. I really am," Tori apologized. "I always thought you were nice, right from the minute I met you. But on the ice I was never able to think of you as a friend—my mother always made me think of you as 'the competition.' "

"You forgot that we're all in this together," Danielle said. "I mean, sure, we have to compete against each other—but we don't have to get so ultraserious and mean."

"Danielle's right," Kathy intervened. "It's one thing to want to do well. But it's another to try to hurt someone else's chances to improve your own. There's no call for that in this club, or at any level, for that matter. So I hope you'll *both* learn how to deal with your competitive sides after this incident," Kathy said. "That kind of behavior won't be tolerated around here. Do you understand, Tori? Everyone?"

Tori nodded. "It won't happen again."

"All right. Make sure of that. But for now—do me a favor and concentrate on passing your tests!" She skated away, leaving the four girls together in the middle of the rink.

Tori glanced nervously at Nikki. "Do you think we can try to be friends again?"

Nikki heard the sincerity in Tori's voice, but she was hesitant. It was hard to forgive her so fast. Nikki had almost quit skating because of Tori.

"She really means it," Danielle said.

"Give her another chance," Jill urged Nikki. "I think you guys understand what's going on now."

"Besides, who else are you going to practice your double flip with?" Tori asked, smiling timidly.

Nikki grinned. "Okay, let's start over."

"I can't believe we both landed our double flips again and passed the test!" Nikki exclaimed to Tori as they both changed out of their skating dresses and into jeans. It was almost two o'clock, and the testing was finally over.

After all that worrying and practicing, the USFSA test had gone very well, Nikki thought. The worst part had been waiting for her turn. The officials had tested about ten skaters, and Nikki had been one of the last to go. She'd also been holding her breath while Tori was tested.

"I know," Tori agreed with a smile. "If you had told me this yesterday, I never would have believed you."

Nikki nodded. Even though she was still uneasy talking to Tori, she had a feeling that soon they'd be good friends. Now that she and Tori were on the same skill level, they would probably have to compete against each other for solos in ice shows and medals in competitions. She hoped they'd handle the situation better from now on; she knew she'd try as hard as she could.

Just then Jill and Danielle ran into the locker room. They showered Nikki and Tori with confetti, shouting "Congratulations!" and "You passed!"

"To show how happy we are that you guys are finally going to be friends and that you both landed your double flips and passed the test," Danielle announced, "we bought you presents in the pro shop."

Jill held her hands behind her back, hiding the presents. "Are you guys ready for this?"

Nikki smiled at Tori as Jill held out their presents— white T-shirts that said "I Flip for Silver Blades" in blue letters. Jill and Danielle had taken a red marker and written in the word *Double,* so the shirts now read "I Double Flip for Silver Blades"!

"These are great—thanks, you guys," Nikki said, holding the shirt up against her body.

"And guess who we saw *in* the pro shop?" Jill asked.

"Hint—he plays hockey, and he's not my obnoxious brother," Danielle said.

"And he asked you to a certain dance we need to put up decorations for, pronto," Jill added.

"No way," Nikki said, shaking her head. "You bumped into Kyle?" Just hearing his name made her nervous. Now that the testing was over, she'd have to tell Kara about her conversation with the hockey player. Kara had probably already called Nikki's house fifty times to find out if he was going to ask her to the dance before tonight.

Nikki glanced at Tori, thinking about how hard it must have been for the other girl to tell the truth earlier today. In spite of everything, Nikki realized, I admire her for speaking up—especially in front of Kathy. Somehow it made what Nikki had to say to Kara seem just a little bit easier.

14

Nikki tried calling Kara's house one more time before leaving for the dance, but no one was home. She hung up on the Logans' answering machine in frustration.

"Hey, Mom," she yelled downstairs. "Are you sure that Kara didn't call me today?"

"Yes, honey, I'm sure," her mother replied.

Nikki wrinkled her nose. She didn't know what to do. She hadn't spoken to Kara all day. That afternoon, while the gym was being decorated, Kara had been bustling all over the room as she supervised things. Nikki had never gotten her alone, and Kara had never asked Nikki about Kyle.

"Oh, well," Nikki mumbled to herself as she brushed her hair one last time. "I guess Kara's figured out by

129

now that Kyle isn't taking her to the dance tonight. I just hope she's not *too* mad at me."

"Those are the most beautiful paper chains I've ever seen. Maybe you guys should give up skating and go into the arts-and-crafts business," Tori teased Nikki, Jill, and Danielle as the four of them walked into the gym.

The other three girls looked at the hundreds of chains covering the ceiling of the school gym and groaned, remembering the hours of cutting and pasting it had taken to create them—and put them up.

"From now on I'll leave making the decorations to other people," Nikki said. She was, though, secretly pleased at how nice the gym looked.

"So this is a Grandview dance?" said Tori, scanning the gym. "Of course, it's not as good as a Kent dance. . . ." She winked at them. "Just kidding. You know, Nikki, you definitely have the best outfit on."

Nikki smiled and looked down at the dark-green minidress Tori had insisted she borrow. It did look good on her.

"Let's just say it's a lot better than that silver-and-gold thing Nikki showed us at the mall last week," Jill said, pointing across the dance floor. They all broke into laughter when they saw a girl wearing the identical shiny outfit.

"Now, what are we going to do?" Danielle asked.

The four girls had been standing in a corner for ten minutes watching everyone dance and eat.

"I suggest we get on that dance floor and show those kids some hot Silver Blades choreography," Jill said, already moving in place to the music.

Nikki had been anxiously scanning the room for Kara. She'd just spotted the other girl standing by the refreshment table. "Could you guys come with me?" she asked. Jill, Danielle, and Tori followed Nikki across the gym.

"Hi," Nikki said, relieved Kara was standing alone. "Just hear me out before you say anything, okay?" She took a deep breath, then plunged in. "I never meant for Kyle to think I wanted to go to the dance with him. And I was never interested in him as a boyfriend, because I knew that you liked him. Jill, Danielle, and Tori will vouch for me—I mentioned your name all the time to Kyle at the rink," said Nikki.

"So many times—it was ridiculous," agreed Danielle. Jill and Tori nodded.

"Everything got messed up with the note," continued Nikki.

"What note?" asked Kara. "What are you talking about?"

"Remember, you told me to do something to get Kyle to ask you to the dance? Well, I left him this note, which was signed 'The president of the dance committee.' I just assumed he'd know that was you. But then Kyle saw me leaving it in his coat. He knew I was on the committee, so yesterday he came up and—"

Nikki stopped explaining, because Kara had burst out laughing. "What's so funny?"

"You're talking about a mile a minute," Kara said. "I can hardly understand you. Anyway, who cares about Kyle? Do you guys see that gorgeous ninth-grader over by the wall—the one with those piercing-blue eyes? Doesn't he look like he should be on TV? I think I'm in love."

Kara trotted off to talk to the blue-eyed ninth-grader, and Nikki was left with her mouth hanging wide open. The other three girls cracked up laughing. "Can you believe that?" Nikki said. "So much for Kara and Kyle!"

"I should have known," said Danielle. "Kara never likes any guy for more than a week."

Jill leaned toward Nikki and whispered: "Kyle is looking at you. I think it's okay for you to like him now."

Nikki blushed. "Like him? Me?"

"Come on, Nikki," said Danielle. "You have to admit he *is* kind of cute."

"Well, now that I think of it . . ." Nikki said.

"Go ask him to dance!" Tori urged.

"Do you think I should?" said Nikki.

Her three friends gently pushed her in Kyle's direction. "Go on!"

Nikki gathered up her courage and walked across the room. Kyle was leaning against the wall, pretending to be fascinated by his shoelaces.

"Hi, Kyle," said Nikki.

"Hi, Nikki," said Kyle.

"Um, want to dance?" asked Nikki.

Kyle looked at her questioningly. "Do you really want to dance with me? Yesterday at the rink you didn't seem too interested."

"Uh," Nikki said. "Well, you see, what happened is . . ." Her voice trailed off as she remembered how frantic she'd been yesterday when she was searching for the videotape and how horrified she'd felt when she'd realized her plan to help Kara had backfired. "I was looking for something, and I guess I was really distracted," she said finally.

"Did you find what you were looking for?" he asked.

Nikki glanced across the dance floor to where her friends were dancing together. Jill winked at her and they all waved.

"Yes," Nikki told Kyle with a grin. "Now can we dance?"

"So did you have fun last night?" Jill asked Nikki as she skated in a circle around her. There was no official practice on Sundays—it was their one day off—but all four girls had decided to meet at the rink anyway during the freestyle session. So far they had the rink to themselves.

"Yeah, I did," Nikki said with a smile. "I was so glad Kara wasn't mad at me about Kyle."

"Kyle was being really funny," Tori said, skating over to Nikki and doing backward crossovers around her. "I like him."

Danielle nodded. She started skating around Nikki too.

"What's going on?" asked Nikki. "Are you guys trying to drive me crazy?"

"No," Jill said. "We just wanted to make sure we had your attention."

"It's time for your official welcome to Silver Blades," Danielle said.

"What are you going to do—splits over my head or something?" Nikki asked.

"No, stupid." Tori held out a small box with red-foil wrap to Nikki. "Open it," she said.

Nikki took the box and removed the ribbon and wrapping paper. Slowly she lifted the lid. Inside the box, lying on a cotton square, was a silver necklace— with a silver skate charm on the end of it, the same as Jill, Danielle, and Tori wore every day. "It's beautiful! Thanks, you guys." Nikki smiled at her three new friends.

"You're welcome," Tori said, smiling back as she came to a stop in front of Nikki. She gave Nikki a brief hug.

"Okay, okay, enough celebrating!" Jill said. "We have a competition coming up, and I for one plan to be ready."

"Let's work on our double flips," Nikki said to Tori as she fastened the necklace around her neck.

"Will you guys help me?" asked Danielle. "I need to land that jump too."

"No problem," Tori said. "Nikki and I are experts. Come on, let's go." She skated off to the other end of the rink.

Nikki looked at Danielle. "We'd better get over there before she chops up all the ice!"

"No kidding," Danielle said as the two of them skated over to join Tori and Jill.

Nikki couldn't help grinning as she watched Tori try her first double flip and then land it on one foot. Welcome to Silver Blades, Nikki told herself.